I0663983

This—
is Murder!

By Cortland FitzSimmons

and

Gerald Adams

Originally published in 1941

This—is Murder!

© 2015 Resurrected Press
www.ResurrectedPress.com

All rights reserved. No part of this book may be used or reproduced in any manner without written permission except for brief quotations for review purposes.

Published by Resurrected Press

This classic book was handcrafted by Resurrected Press. Resurrected Press is dedicated to bringing high quality classic books back to the readers who enjoy them. These are not scanned versions of the originals, but, rather, quality checked and edited books meant to be enjoyed!

Please visit ResurrectedPress.com to view our entire catalogue, and like us on Facebook at Facebook.com/ResurrectedPress to stay updated!

ISBN 13: 978-1-943403-03-5

Printed in the United States of America

Resurrected Press Books in *The Ethel Thomas Detective Story* Series by Cortland Fitzsimmons

The Whispering Window
The Moving Finger
Mystery at Hidden Harbor
The Evil Men Do

Other books by Cortland Fitzsimmons

The Manville Murders
The Bainbridge Murder
No Witness!
Red Rhapsody
Sudden Silence
One Man's Poison
This—is Murder!

Resurrected Press Books in *The Chief Inspector Pointer Mystery* <u>Series</u>

RESURRECTED PRESS CLASSIC
MYSTERY CATALOGUE

Journeys into Mystery
Travel and Mystery in a More Elegant Time

The Edwardian Detectives
Literary Sleuths of the Edwardian Era

Gems of Mystery
Lost Jewels from a More Elegant Age

Anne Austin
One Drop of Blood
The Black Pigeon
Murder at Bridge

E. C. Bentley
Trent's Last Case: The Woman in Black

Ernest Bramah
Max Carrados Resurrected:
The Detective Stories of Max Carrados

Agatha Christie
The Secret Adversary
The Mysterious Affair at Styles

Octavus Roy Cohen
Midnight

Freeman Wills Croft
The Ponson Case
The Pit Prop Syndicate

The Uttermost Farthing: A Savant's Vendetta

Arthur Griffiths
The Passenger From Calais
The Rome Express

Fergus Hume
The Mystery of a Hansom Cab
The Green Mummy
The Silent House
The Secret Passage

Edgar Jepson
The Loudwater Mystery

A. E. W. Mason
At the Villa Rose

A. A. Milne
The Red House Mystery

Baroness Emma Orczy
The Old Man in the Corner

Edgar Allan Poe
The Detective Stories of Edgar Allan Poe

Arthur J. Rees
The Hampstead Mystery
The Shrieking Pit
The Hand In The Dark
The Moon Rock
The Mystery of the Downs

Mary Roberts Rinehart
Sight Unseen and The Confession

Dorothy L. Sayers

Whose Body?

Sir William Magnay
The Hunt Ball Mystery

Mabel and Paul Thorne
The Sheridan Road Mystery

Louis Tracy
The Strange Case of Mortimer Fenley
The Albert Gate Mystery
The Bartlett Mystery
The Postmaster's Daughter
The House of Peril
The Sandling Case: What Would You Have Done?

Charles Edmonds Walk
The Paternoster Ruby

John R. Watson
The Mystery of the Downs
The Hampstead Mystery

Edgar Wallace
The Daffodil Mystery
The Crimson Circle

Carolyn Wells
Vicky Van
The Man Who Fell Through the Earth
In the Onyx Lobby
Raspberry Jam
The Clue
The Room with the Tassels
The Vanishing of Betty Varian
The Mystery Girl
The White Alley
The Curved Blades

Anybody but Anne
The Bride of a Moment
Faulkner's Folly
The Diamond Pin
The Gold Bag
The Mystery of the Sycamore
The Come Back

Raoul Whitfield
Death in a Bowl

And much more!
Visit ResurrectedPress.com
for our complete catalogue

*LIKE us on Facebook for upcoming release
announcements!*

Facebook.com/ResurrectedPress

FOREWORD

One of the first pieces of advice to budding authors is to write about what you know. The authors of *This–is Murder!* certainly took that to heart when they wrote the mystery which is set on a yacht off of Catalina during a publicity junket for an upcoming film. Cortland Fitzsimmons had already had a decade long career writing screenplays, many of which were based on his novels. Gerald Adams was just beginning his career as a screenwriter, but he would go on to write for some of the best known TV series of the '50s and '60s as well as numerous movies including several staring Elvis Presley.

There's also no doubt that from the start the authors wrote the mystery with the idea of turning it into a movie. All the elements of a classic black and white movie mystery from the 1930s are present; the snappy dialog, the cast of stock characters, an element of romance. As one reads *This–is Murder!*, it doesn't take much imagination to conjure of the images of the film that might have been. The action from the murder to the final confrontation is quite intentionally very visual in it nature.

Light hearted mystery films were a popular staple of Hollywood during the 1930s and 1940s. Dashiell Hammett's novel *The Thin Man* was turned into a popular series of films starring William Powell and Myrna Loy, and such well known actors as Bob Hope, Red Skelton, and Jack Benny all used the mystery genre for some of their feature films in the era. *This–is Murder!* is certainly cast in that mold.

Fitzsimmons was certainly familiar with the formula. Many of the films that he worked on were mysteries based on novels that he wrote. His specialty was setting the mystery against some aspect of popular culture such as sports or the music business. He got his start in the film business when his mystery *70,000 Witnesses: A Football Mystery* was turned into a film. This was followed shortly by *Death on the Diamond: a Baseball Mystery*. He worked on other screenplays for mysteries throughout the 1930s as well as a number of novels that could quite easily have been turned into films. Adams, who had worked as a literary agent was just getting started as a writer, but given his later success he learned quickly.

The setting for *This–is Murder!* is a yacht anchored off of Catalina Island that is being used for a publicity party for some of the cast and crew of an upcoming movie *Blue Lagoon*. All the usual suspects are there, the producer, the director, the handsome leading man, the exotic leading lady, her main rival at the studio, as well as a number of former and current lovers of the leading lady. When she is murdered, the screenwriter on the film must turn amateur detective as the yacht becomes isolated and fog bound with only his girl-friend and the local beach cop to help him.

This–is Murder! is an entertaining mystery written by a pair of talented professionals who knew how to work the genre for all it was worth. Fictional Press is pleased to bring its readers who love old black and white films this new edition of *This–is Murder!*

About the Authors

Cortland Fitzsimmons was born in Brooklyn, New York (possibly Queens) on June 19, 1893 and died July 25, 1949 in Los Angeles, California. After attending New York University and The City College of New York, he worked for some time as a salesman for several book distributors and publishers before turning to writing full time in 1934. Most of his works as a writer were mysteries, a number of which were based on sports themes such as *70,000 Witnesses: A Football Mystery,* *Crimson Ice: A Hockey Mystery,* and *Death on a Diamond: A Baseball Mystery.* A number of his novels were made into films and he moved to Los Angeles to work as a screenwriter. His last book was a cookbook that he co-wrote with his wife Muriel Simpson *You Can Cook If You Can Read.*

Gerald Drayson Adams (June 25, 1900-August 23, 1988) Born in Winnipeg, Canada, Adams was educated at Oxford and was a former businessman and literary agent before turning to screenwriting in the '40s. He continued to write for both the films and television into the mid '60s. While mostly known for his work on action and adventure films, he also was involved in to movies featuring Elvis Presley, *Kissin' Cousins* and *Harum Scarum.* He also wrote screenplays for the TV series *including Maverick, Surfside 6, and Northwest Passage.*

Greg Fowlkes
Editor-In-Chief
Resurrected Press
www.ResurrectedPress.com
Facebook.com/ResurrectedPress

CHAPTER ONE

THE *Parrakeet*, MY fifty-foot cruiser — in my more expansive moments I have been known to refer to her as a yacht — was riding peacefully at anchor off Catalina Island, just north of the Casino. I was apparently doing absolutely nothing stretched out comfortably in my pajamas on some cushions aft; on what Shanghai — my Peke — considered his private patrol deck. Actually I was gathering the threads of a plot prior to writing another of what the critics, in their quaint way, are apt to call another of Mallory's alleged mystery novels.

The deep-throated whistle of the Mainland boat boomed across the harbor and bounced back from the rocky walls of the Island. She was about to leave for the night. I didn't have to raise my head to know that, for coming across the water I could hear the tinkle of the steel-guitars and the softly sad strains of *Aloha*, which is always sung as the steamer departs A nice custom swiped from Hawaii without the benefit of ASCAP, but still good.

Gulls wheeled and cried overhead, either in annoyance or expectancy, as they circled toward the steamer. There was the hushed murmur of farewells and another blast from the boat. I could hear her screws churning the water, knew that she had nosed out to sea and I was glad that the Island was to settle down for the night.

I could hear Lee Wing in the galley washing up the dinner dishes prior to going ashore for his nightly bout with the marble machines. I was feeling rather pleased with myself as I sipped my after-dinner liqueur, satisfied that for once in my life I would and could do exactly as I pleased. I had had a long swim in the late afternoon and had loafed ever since. Hollywood and the studio were safely on the Mainland, my trials and tribulations were a thing of the past. The *Parrakeet* rocked soothingly with the gentle swell created by the passing of the steamer. The short period of dusk was fading rapidly.

Lee Wing came on deck and fixed the riding-light at the mast, brought me another pillow for my head, then touched me for a further advance on his salary before taking the dingy to head for the marble games ashore.

A little later I was watching the after-sunset glow when suddenly my vision of pinks, violets, and burning gold was cut off by a white hull gliding by.

Being a writer I'm considerably curious and rolled over on an elbow to gaze up at the magnificent yacht which was dwarfing the *Parrakeet* as she slipped by, ghostlike in the gathering gloom. So much for curiosity. They might have spotted the *Parrakeet* anyhow, I don't know, but they did see me and that was that.

"DEAN MALLORY . . . AHOY!"

I tried to duck out of sight but it was a futile effort, for leaning over the rail stood a short, fat, bald-headed man obviously yelling at me. It was Sid Tricker, my boss— President of Tricker Pictures Incorporated, known about Hollywood as Tricker's Flickers. He had bought my latest novel—*Blue Lagoon*—had made it possible for me to get the *Parrakeet* out of hock and do a number of other things I had been delaying for just such a windfall. I yelled back.

"'LO! SID. WHAT THE HELL'RE YOU DOING HERE?"

"BIG PARTY TONIGHT. COME OVER."

"SORRY—I'M BUSY. BESIDES, I'VE BEEN ON YOUR PARTIES."

"WRITING?"

"NO. THINKING—YOU APE."

"COME OVER ANYWAY. YOU NEED EXCITEMENT."

"KEEP GOING!"

I was tired of shouting, gave him a fadeout signal and returned to my liqueur. Shanghai had lapped a good inch off the top of it—he gazed owlishly up at me and said,

"Whurps!"

He was bleary. He yawned, I yawned back at him. He stuck his head between his paws and fell asleep— so did I. Fell asleep, I mean.

When I woke up it was dark. Someone was calling my name and shaking my shoulder. I opened an eye, liked what I saw—it was Victoria Blaire, my one weakness, a piquant brunette. Beautiful? I thought so, anyway, and called her Vicky.

She said, "So this is how you work on a new novel!"

"I let the subconscious plot for me," I explained with a pleased smile.

"So that's what's wrong with 'em," she said.

"I—" I was going to retort but decided to ignore the crack.

I was glad to see Vicky, and a little annoyed, not because she had come to call on me on the *Parrakeet* but because she had undoubtedly come to the Island with Sid Tricker's party.

"Why the gloom?" she demanded.

"You," I replied flatly. "You're with Tricker, aren't you?"

I hadn't seen her for two days, thought she was busy designing costumes at the studio for *Blue Lagoon*— and yet, if I remember my story correctly, that shouldn't have taken long.

"He's my boss, isn't he?" she demanded. "I'm working for him, am I not? I need the job, don't I?"

"I know a chap who would like to keep you in the manner to which you think you are accustomed," I replied. "You wouldn't have to work or go on Hollywood parties then."

"Thanks for the proposal, Dean. That's one sweet thing about you—you're consistent, I'll say that for you."

"It's about the hundredth time I've proposed to you."

"Only the twenty-third if you want to be exact. Are you going to get up?"

"Not until you say you'll marry me."

"You're going to look funny going around on the flat of your back," she retorted. "Look, Dean, let's not get into an argument about that again. I want you to come over to the yacht."

"Not me!" I exploded. "I came over here to get away from the studio and that crowd."

"Please, Dean. I'm afraid."

I jerked to attention at that, swung my legs down from the cushions and looked up at her. "Who is he? I'll knock his block off," I promised.

"It isn't a man, Dean. It's the whole party. I wish to heaven I had stayed home!"

"I don't get it. What's the matter with the party?"

"That's what I don't know. There's something going on. It's like the beginning of one of your stories. There's something in the air, odd people doing odd things. There's hate and fury, leashed now, but ready to break out at any moment. Of course, Zara Murza is aboard and Queen of the party, and I mean Queen. It's a publicity stunt for her. Naomi Ravelle is there too, and when they look at each other fire darts from their eyes. There's a rajah, a dark, oily-looking man who is supposed to own the yacht. There's that rug peddler and the big Russian Sarakov, and Frank Lane looking as if he'd like to knife everybody just for the fun of it and a man by the name of Grey who looks like a firecracker with the fuse burned out."

"The rug peddler?" I asked. "Who is he?"

"You'll know him when you see him. He haunts the studios. His name is Zamper and when he walks he looks like a croquet wicket."

I laughed. I had seen the man with the openwork legs.

"Don't laugh, Dean. It's a horrible party. I tell you I'm afraid to stay on board."

That was an odd admission coming from her. She had plenty of nerve; I'd seen her in action. "I'll put you up at the St. Catharine or you can marry me and stay here," I suggested.

"That's twenty-four," she said. "Thanks. I suppose I

sound like a nitwit, Dean, but I don't want to miss any of it. I'm morbidly fascinated."

"Why should I try to figure out a plot for a new novel when you have just given me a load of material? I'll put some clothes on and go back with you," I said, curious myself.

"You're dressed," she said. She meant my pajamas, which were the smock type. "This is an Oriental costume party in honor of the Rajah. Just put on that robe and you're ready."

She pointed to my gorgeous Mandarin robe which Shang had given me for Christmas. It was red with gold dragons cruising around on the surface. I climbed into it and led her toward the dingy.

I tossed the Peke in after her and climbed down myself.

Vicky rowed. This is one of the many things I like about her—whatever she does she does well. I have spent many pleasant hours cogitating on what a wonderful wife she'd be—when I could finally persuade her to say Yes. I looked ahead at the yacht; her white sides gleamed with the reflected lights from the shore. Her portholes glowed, there was the sound of music and laughter—you know the kind that comes after several drinks, high, hollow and empty.

Suddenly I regretted leaving the *Parrakeet*. "Take me back," I said.

"No."

"Look, Vicky! You won't marry me because you think I'm going to become a drunkard. Is that right?"

'That's three reasons," she agreed.

"And the three times that I've been tight in my whole life were the three times you happened to see me."

"Happened to see you," she scoffed. "I couldn't miss you. You acted like a veteran."

"And you're pulling too hard on the port oar— precious," I said, giving vent to my pique that way.

"And *I'm* rowing this barge," she retorted in her best

fireside manner.

"And I've explained to you twenty-four times that a Hollywood party does things to me, drives me to drink. They do something to me, Vicky," I repeated, "and, I warn you, you're leading me to drink right now."

"You've heard about the horse and the trough, haven't you?" she snapped back, heaved hard on her port oar but not in time to keep us from bumping into the yacht. She made the painter fast before the deckhand scampered down to help. She reached down for Shang, tucked him under her arm and said, "Come on, Weak-will."

"Well! Look who's here!" Sid Tricker called as we hit the deck. He gave me the double O—so did everyone else. "Who you supposed to be—Fu Manchu?" he asked.

I could see that the costumes weren't much. I told him I wasn't quite sure but would let him know later when I made up my mind. At that moment the Hollywood pest arrived—Betty Potter, star reporter for the New York *Sphere*—a lady who knew more about your business than you did yourself.

"Why, Mr. Mallory—of all things!" she gushed. She's a bit of a fountain and casts off fine spray. "I do declare! What an original idea for a costume, and so simple too! That's my favorite shade of red too—and those gold cats. . . ." She stood off, pretending to admire the robe, but there was a gimlet quality about her eyes which made me nervous, conscious of my pajamas and not quite sure that I was completely covered.

"Dragons," I corrected and tightened my sash. It was futile, however, to correct her. She was never very near the truth and seemed to thrive on it.

"That's right, so they are. Must make a note of it for my column. Now you must let me introduce you to the Rajah."

She loved doing things like that. The bigger the shot, the happier Betty could be. She swung around and looked like what the well-dressed harem belle should avoid. She was very heavy in the rift, if you know what I mean. The next moment her claws dug into my arm. Some day when I've made all the money I can in Hollywood I'll probably break her column— spinal.

"Oh, Ra-aj!" she cooed in her mock-honey voice which was supposed to suggest familiarity.

A tall dark-skinned man wearing a turban and evening clothes turned from a group to look down his nose at us.

"Raj—this is Dean Mallory, the author."

I had made up my mind to kick her in the shins if she called me a writer.

"Glad to meet you," I said.

He said, "Have a drink."

"Now it commences," I whispered to Vicky.

"Be a horse," she threw back.

The Rajah had clapped his hands and a tray full of drinks arrived. We hoisted a couple of long green ones, told each other what swell fellows we were—then I pushed off in search of Vicky, who had deserted me. I was thinking of that crack of hers about the horse and took just a few sips before parking my glass in the first convenient spot.

I finally located her. She was sitting on a settee in the stern. The Peke was in her lap. I sat down beside her.

I said, "Looks like a swell party—when're we going to get married?"

She had beautiful turquoise-green eyes that slanted up at the ends. She turned them on me and said, "When you quit drinking. Nice crowd here, don't you think, or don't you?"

"I wouldn't know—besides, I'm not a drinking man, except on occasions," I replied, wondering why women always want to make a man over.

"You ought to see yourself when you've got a skinful," she suggested graphically.

"I try not to."

She wrinkled her little nose at me—she always did that when she was mad. She picked up the Peke and walked away.

I looked around at the guests—I knew most of them. The whole cast from *Blue Lagoon* seemed to be on board, probably another of Sid's famous publicity stunts. He came over and parked the carcass beside me. He was doing his best to seem on top of the world.

"Going to be a great party, Dean—swell publicity," he bragged.

I agreed that it probably was but asked, "Why the Rajah?"

"Hasn't been pulled for a long time. It was my own idea," he boasted.

"Better mark it down then—it's your first," I quipped.

He looked pained. He prodded a stubby forefinger into my navel, an annoying habit of his.

"You don't understand, Dean. This is the biggest thing in the history of the motion picture business. Listen! I hire the yacht—and it cost me pu-lenty. I got the Rajah from Central Casting—ten bucks a day. And I got Betty Potter. Don't tell her it's phony. She's going to give the thing a big write-up in the New York papers—besides, her stuffs syndicated all over the country. The story will be that this egg is the Rajah of Benang—owns an island off the coast of China, or India—I forget which."

"Better make up your mind, and stick to it," I advised.

"Anyway his island has lots of lagoons. He's supposed to be so taken with the sterling integrity of Tricker Pictures that he has offered us his island and the famous Benang dancing girls—than which there are none whicher—to help make *Blue Lagoon* the picture of the century. Of course, we'll shoot it down near Ensenada, but it'll look like the real goods—clean romance of the South Seas. What do you think of that—eh?"

He asked the question so confidently that I could not resist the impulse to rag him. I held my nose and replied, "I think it smells."

Sid immediately rebelled.

"That's the trouble with you, Dean. You're a nice

fellow, but you think you're the only one with brains. All you writers are alike. Why?"

I told him that we had to do that to keep men like him impressed, that we did have brains or he wouldn't hire us. I liked to get his goat. But he looked so crestfallen that I felt sorry immediately. "Don't pay any attention to the things I say, Sid. It's wise-cracking Hollywood stuff. A habit a chap gets into in self-defense. It's a swell party and I hope you get all the publicity out of it you want."

"It's ain't such a swell party, Dean. I've been trying to kid myself about it. I'm worried."

That was the second time the words were used in connection with the party. "What's up?" I asked.

"Something's wrong with the crowd. It's what you fellows that write would have words for to explain. It's the uninvited guest — remember you used the words in one of your books?"

"Who is it? Throw him out," I suggested.

"It ain't a real person, Dean. It's a feeling I have. Things are going on. I don't feel comfortable; the party ain't going right. Maybe the goddamn tub is haunted, I don't know."

I laughed. I couldn't help it. Sid trying to express himself in that way was funny. His suggestion that the yacht was haunted had possibilities, however.

"Don't laugh," he begged. "I'm glad you came aboard. I feel better with you here. I can trust you, Dean."

"It's swell of you to say that, Sid. I appreciate it."

"I mean it. You're a screwball, all writers are nuts, but you're a nice kind of a nut. I know when you're laughing at me, you ain't mean, you don't do it behind my back. Stick around, will you?"

"Sure. Glad to. If you need any help, let me know. I've been spoiling for a fight for a long time."

"No! Dean, no! No more fights."

"Has there been one already?" I asked with some regret.

"Didn't you hear about last night at Ciro's? No, you

were over here. Anyhow I hope I've hushed it up. A man
by the name of Grey and the Russian Sarakov had a
row—over Zara," he added. "Now they're both on board—
she made me ask them, said it was the only way to kill
the story if it should leak out. There's something
brewing—what it is I dunno."

A lovely golden arm slid around Sid's neck. It
belonged to Zara Murza—the exotic, beautiful leading
lady of Tricker Pictures and Sid's own particular head
ache. Sid went mute. He scowled a warning for silence at
me.

She said, "Sid darling—run along now, I want to talk
to Dean."

He seemed relieved and pushed off muttering to
himself. Zara flowed into the spot he'd vacated. She was a
true daughter of Romany; her lustrous dark eyes were as
soft as velvet; her hair—jet-black with intriguing blue
lights; her face—oval with the perfect features of a Benda
mask; and her body—a poem of rippling beauty. In other
words, she was pretty much the berries—but I try not to
pick 'em, the dark kind. A fellow's apt to get stuck. I'd
found that out.

She wore an extremely low-cut, white silk dancing
dress that almost didn't quite cover; white brocaded
slippers encased her small feet, and her arms were a
mass of glittering bracelets. I suppose she was done up as
a nautch girl for the Rajah's benefit or possibly her own.
She never missed a trick.

She dipped the tips of her lacquered fingers daintily
into the cocktail she carried, lifted out the cherry and put
it between my lips. That wasn't so bad for a beginning. I
munched it thoughtfully and waited for the next act. I
like cherries. Presently the next move came.

"You don't like me—do you, Dean?"

I said, "I wouldn't put it quite like that but the answer
is no."

Her eyes grew wide and dreamy.

"And why? Am I too mysterious or is it that you are

afraid of me?"

"Maybe I understand you. And as far as your mystery goes—in that dress! Why don't you try cellophane, it's much more concealing."

She laughed musically. "Then you do like it?"

"I'm afraid of it—if you cough you'll bust up the party."

"It is not so," she said and frowned prettily. She took a deep breath to demonstrate the strength of the dress. I looked away and saw Vicky leaning against the rail pretending to talk to Frank Lane, but her eyes were on us. It pleased me to think she might be jealous.

Frank Lane was Sid's top director. I like Frank, he's a nice fellow, but there's only one Vicky, and Frank has had a reputation as a heart-breaker. I gave her a dirty look. I was jealous myself. She put out her tongue at me. I looked down at Zara, who had missed all the little byplay. She was still holding her breath for my benefit—the shoulder-straps were under a heavy strain but were holding their own bravely. I patted her on the back for Vicky's benefit.

"That's swell—you must have a good dressmaker—you can let it out now."

She was like a child. She let her breath ease out with a long sighing sound that was meant to be captivating.

"Are you satisfied now, Mr. Man?" she asked, showing her too white teeth.

I told her that I supposed I was, but to be careful.

Just then Basil St. Denis, her leading man, came over. He was tall, blond, handsome, and more than a bit conceited. I excused myself and went over to Vicky.

I draped myself on the rail. She looked up and said, "You would have to butt in just when Frank is telling me what beautiful eyes I have—didn't you, Frank?"

Frank took a sip at his highball and said, "Yes—I did. Y'know, Dean, she ought to be in pictures—she'd photograph like a million dollars—she's got a figure that'd make even the gorgeous Zara jealous."

I gulped. I must have been overlooking things. I had always regarded Vicky as a darn sweet kid—which she was, and clever too. I didn't enjoy having other people pointing out her physical perfections to me. It didn't seem quite decent, but I looked the situation over and rubbed my eyes. The little devil had on a dress that was almost a duplicate of the one that Zara was wearing and every bit as revealing, if not more so.

I grabbed her by the arm and started along the deck. She instantly gave tongue. "Hey! You big sap—where d'you think you're going?"

"Your dress has done things to me. Where's your cabin?"

"Number Four on this side, but it doesn't mean a thing to you. Let go of me!"

I found the cabin and shoved her in, then slammed the door shut behind me.

"Now," I said, "where're your clothes?"

She sat on the bed and wrinkled her nose at me.

"What clothes? I've only got slacks and a sweater with me besides what I've got on."

I found some slacks and things on a chair and tossed them at her.

"Take off that yard of silk and get respectable."

I was seeing red. It's all right for a dame like Zara to show all she owns, that's part of her business; but Vicky—well, I felt that she was definitely my business. I'd been on enough parties that start out all right and end up all wrong, and call me what you will, I had a hunch about that party. I hadn't seen much, but what I had seen I didn't like, and what I'd heard about it had made it even less attractive. No, that isn't exactly true. I might have liked it all except for the fact that Vicky was aboard; that gave everything a new tone. God knows I'm no Saint Anthony and have never made any pretenses on that score but I guess every guy, no matter what he is or does, has one citadel that he wants to keep unsullied. Vicky was mine.

I was thinking about the motley crew aboard. I'd seen enough from the corner of my eye to know that they were a rum bunch, a gang that would quite easily spell trouble wherever they were if things went rolling. Zara too. She had never bothered to turn her spot on me in public before, and knowing that baby, I had a hunch that her attention had a double purpose. She never did anything without a good reason. She had flirted with me to bait some poor devil and it was quite likely that a row might follow if there was more of the flirtation.

I had just about made up my mind to kidnap Vicky, take her ashore and put her up at the St. Catharine. Later I wished I had. Anyhow I didn't do it at the moment, and you know once a moment has passed it is gone for good. She had been sitting there looking at me resentfully and that got my goat. I saw red again.

"Get going!" I ordered.

She was stubborn. She threw the clothes I had tossed at her on the floor and said, "I won't!"

I gave a hitch to the Mandarin robe and said, "Okay, precious—if you won't—then Daddy will."

She stood up and said with tantalizing defiance, "Is that so?"

I told her that it was—gave one tug at the flimsy stuff and the costume ripped off.

I was sorry and ashamed the moment I had done it, and afraid I'd ruined things for us. Her slip was scanty but she didn't seem to be aware of that as she eyed me coldly.

"Put 'em on, will you?" I begged, pointing to the slacks, and went outside.

I waited a long time, anxiously—wondering what she would say if and when she came out, what I could say to square myself with her. Finally she called matter-of-factly, "You can come in now."

I stood just inside the door, noted she was humming, seemed happy about something. I told her I was sorry.

She looked at me. "I'm glad you are because that was

a lovely dress—it was so beautiful, and expensive, and now it's ruined."

I began to feel very lousy about the whole thing. She was a darling and I loved her, and I was sorry that I'd torn the damn dress and I'd told her so, but I knew I'd do it again and I told her that too. I didn't care how much Zara was ogled or anyone else, for that matter, but I'd be damned if I'd let them ogle Vicky.

"I'm very sorry, precious—but I won't have the girl I'm going to marry make a show of herself before a bunch of Hollywood stallions."

She dabbed at her eyes with a tiny lace handkerchief.

"I wasn't." She actually started to cry. "I put it on for you and no one else, and . . ."

"Damn!" I took her by the arm, opened the cabin door and pushed her through.

We bumped into Betty Potter. She would have to be there. After all—there are times when we should not meet people.

She was looking past us into the cabin. Her eyes seemed to gasp before she turned them on me.

"Oh, oh! Mr. Mallory—naughty-naughty."

I looked back—on the floor, in full view, lay the torn dress and it looked . . . Well, Betty had decided how it looked. Our reputations were shot.

I stalked past her, dragging Vicky with me. We were just another couple of saps, as far as Betty Potter was concerned, and she thought she had a finger on us, thanks to that damned dress and my sudden surge of righteousness. It would be no use trying to explain to her that nothing had happened. The thing looked like hell; she had made up her mind—it was a foul mind, anyway.

Since I had started out to protect Vicky and had made a mess of it I decided to see to it that nothing further would happen to her. All Betty had to do was to drop a hint to those boulevard Casanovas of what she thought had happened and they would be around Vicky in droves.

Coiled on the top of a life-boat I found a length of

rope. I picked it up, tied one end around Vicky's waist and the other about my own.

I said, "There now—you stick with me until this party's over."

She looked up at me and smiled.

"You're a good scout, Dean," she said. "I feel so safe with you—you treat me like a sister."

I kissed her and said, "Won't any more."

I was startled by a sudden smack. It seemed like a mockery of our kiss and I was ready to fight. I was wrong. The sound I had heard was the sharp impact of a hand on flesh. A man reeled out of a companion-way holding his hand to his face. He was dressed as an Arab chieftain; his turban had slipped down and I didn't see his face but I made up my mind to watch out for a black eye.

"The business of the evening seems to be beginning," Vicky said and led me toward the bar, of all places.

CHAPTER TWO

THE BAR WAS DOing a flourishing business. We pried open a space at the rail and pushed it. I ordered a celery tonic for myself and a silver fizz for Vicky.

She gasped, "Don't be a fool!"

"Listen, light of my life, I'm trying to exercise control. You know how easy it is to drink on one of these parties."

"And you ought to know when to stop," she said. "You can drink without getting drunk, can't you?"

"Normally, yes, but not on these parties. There's something about talking, with no one listening to what you have to say, that's unnerving. The habit these charming people have of breaking into a sentence to make some remark of their own grates on my nerves. My head is full of broken sentences, unfinished thoughts, devastated conversations. I drink in self-defense and now when I'm trying to show you how strong I am, what a horse I have become, you, of all people, scoff at me."

"You ought to be used to Hollywood conversations by now," she said. "Why try to talk to people who don't listen? Just say a few words now and then, crib a joke from the *New Yorker*, repeat a Marx story and you'll be labeled a brilliant conversationalist."

The man next to me turned and asked, "Aren't you Dean Mallory?"

I agreed that I was and took a good look at him. He was the Arab chief and his eye was not black, but his face had a spot of high color.

"Hell, Mr. Grey—haven't seen you in a coon's age," I said, trying to be affable.

The man was Henry Grey—tall, handsome and distinguished—President of the Grey Air Lines. I had met him before on a few parties the previous fall.

"Nice party," he tossed back.

"Very."

He nodded vaguely and his eyes wandered off to where a few couples were dancing on the deck. I followed his gaze. He seemed unable to take his eyes off Zara. She was dancing with Basil St. Denis. They made a striking pair—he so tall and blond, she so petite and dark. Grey muttered something that I didn't catch and sauntered onto the deck. A little later I saw him dancing with Zara, their heads close together in conversation. St. Denis didn't seem too pleased with the situation.

I took a good look at the girls about me. It was a brunette evening—a new era in Hollywood. About the only blonde on board of any importance was that dizzy pest Betty Potter, and she was a manufactured one. I know about that because 1 accidentally saw her taking a sun bath once—her sun tent blew over at Palm Springs and I had to help disentangle her. I've avoided Palm Springs ever since.

I took a sip of my celery tonic. It was horrible.

Naomi Ravelle—a dusky Spanish beauty who'd been slated for the lead in *Blue Lagoon* until Zara came on the scene—joggled my arm and said, "Hallo."

I said, "Hello, Naomi!"

She said, "Let's dance."

I said, "Can't—tied up all evening," and pointed to the rope.

Vicky walked away to talk to somebody and the rope jerked me off the rail. My drink splashed. Naomi laughed. I borrowed a towel and wiped celery tonic off my Mandarin robe and then pulled on the rope. Vicky was immediately by my side again, bringing a friend with her. Her friend turned out to be Michael Sarakov, the Russian, an enormous fellow, with a shock of iron-gray hair topping a strong, heavily bronzed face. He spoke faultless English with just a trace of accent.

He said, "This is a great pleasure, Mr. Mallory. I have always enjoyed reading your stories."

Of course I liked that. I said thanks and would he care for a drink? He would—a Scotch and soda. I ordered one. "Miss Blaire has told me a great deal about you, Mr. Mallory."

"Then you'd better forget it—Vicky has a great imagination."

"Is that so? I told Michael that you were a grand person—but I didn't mean a word of it, so there!"

The big Russian smiled and spoke softly.

"You also said, Miss Blaire, that you were in love with Mr. Mallory—you did not mean that either?"

Vicky blushed; before she could make a reply Betty Potter crashed in. She was pretty well boiled.

"Oh. Hallo, everybody! What's all the powwow about? Have I missed anything?"

I said, "If you have it isn't your fault."

Sarakov was more polite.

"I was just asking Miss Blaire if it was true that she loved Mr. Mallory," he explained.

"Is it true! Well, I hope to tell you! If you'd seen what I saw . . . *Ouch!*"

I had stepped on her foot and whispered a warning into her ear. I must have looked ferocious. She hobbled off without another word.

"You are a genius to be able to do that," he said.

Vicky asked, "What did you say to her?"

"Palm Springs."

"What's that got to do with it?"

"Nothing much. It's her secret. Let's go on deck."

Sarakov mumbled something and moved away. He had been like a specter at a feast as he had talked to us. His words had come glibly enough but neither his mind nor his attention was on us. His eyes had followed Zara as she swayed in Grey's arms. His great head had moved in unison with their rhythm.

Vicky looked after him. "He had a row with Grey in Ciro's last night. It was over your friend Zara," she said.

"He's been watching them since they started to dance.

Come on, if there's going to be anything interesting I want to see it," I suggested. "I haven't seen anything yet that explains why both you and Sid feel squirmish."

A five-piece string orchestra, perched atop the boat deck, was playing a rhumba as we emerged from the bar and found a vacant settee near the port rail. Dancing isn't one of my fortes; I like to watch from the side lines and endeavor to classify what each swirling couple have on their minds—if they have any—usually it isn't a very difficult feat. Sid Tricker was standing a few feet away talking to Frank Lane, rubbing his hands together nervously—he always did that when he was excited. I gathered that another of his hot publicity ideas was about to pollute the atmosphere.

I was right.

The Rajah came stalking down the deck; light from the waving Japanese lanterns which had sprung into being, reflected glowingly in the huge jewel that he wore in his turban.

When he had reached the center of the dancing floor he turned to the orchestra and held up his hand commandingly. The music ceased instantly. He turned to the guests.

"My friends," he said in an ultra-Oxonian accent—Sid sure knew his extras—"as you all know, I am giving this party in honor of the queen of all that is beautiful —for Zara, the lovely lady who will shortly grace the shores of my beautiful Benang where the picture *Blue Lagoon* will be filmed by that genius of the age—Mr. Sid Tricker."

I could see Sid's chest stick out as he looked proudly over at Betty Potter, who was doing her stuff with pad and pencil. Meanwhile the Rajah had walked over to Zara and bowed. From his pocket he took a long velvet jewel case. He opened it and took out an enormous rope of pearls and held them for everyone to admire.

She actually said, "For me?" as her eyes gloated over them.

Leave it to Sid to get the biggest ones he could find —

he'd have used billiard balls if he could have got away with it. He glanced over triumphantly at me. I signaled hearty approval by holding my nose. He looked away quickly.

Satisfied that everyone had got a good eyeful of the pearls, the Rajah continued: "A necklace of pink pearls — the only jewels fit for your matchless beauty." He placed the necklace around her throat and snapped the clasp.

A lot of Ohs and Ahs came from the envious ladies present, who began to wonder what Zara had that they lacked.

Zara accepted them with flashing eyes, there was nothing she loved better than to be the center of things, particularly when the graft was good. I felt sorry for Sid when she found out that it was all a publicity stunt, and the pearls only genuine Western Costume baubles —she'd tear him apart. The music started again, the deck filled with dancers. Zara blissed away in the arms of the Rajah, giving as much as she could at the moment. I flagged Sid.

"What's the matter, Dean?" he asked, resting on the arm of the settee. Before I could reply Vicky opened up.

"1 think this is all too wonderful for words—like a dream out of the Arabian Nights," she cried.

Sid looked funny for a moment. I guess he thought he was being kidded, but Vicky was staring enraptured into space. She was really a very clever girl. It finally went over with Sid and he warmed up.

"You ain't seen nothin' yet. Wait for the next surprise," he bubbled.

I yawned and said it would probably be terrific.

His eyes snapped.

"You ain't kidding me—are you, Dean?"

I shook my head. "No—neither will Zara when she finds out this is only a publicity stunt and the Rajah can be had for ten bucks a day."

Vicky said, "Oh!" as if the world had suddenly gone dark and dreary. She gave Sid a hurt accusing look. Sid began to look thoughtful with something real to worry about.

"I want to go home," Vicky said.

"Why, beautiful?" I said, forgetting all about Sid. "You know you can't walk, and, things being as they are, you can't stay on the *Parrakeet.*"

"I want to go home anyhow. I was having such a swell time, thinking it was all real, and now . . ." Her voice trailed away as she became interested in Zara and Betty Potter standing a few feet away from us. Vicky gasped, and I didn't wonder. Zara gave Potter a resounding smack right across the kisser, as they say over on Tenth Avenue. It was a honey and made me feel good. It was just the thing Betty needed, but a movie actress or a writer is not exactly the person to violate the royal Potter carcass; that is, if they hope to make peanut money in Hollywood. The Potter girl is dynamite and while I would like to see her blow up I'm not the man to light the fuse; not yet at any rate, I want a few more years in Hollywood. It's made me soft, I like my boat and the creature comforts Cinemaland has given me, and I like the town; it's no crazier than any other place, just more concentrated, that's all.

Poor Sid! I'd forgotten about him for the moment. He'd been cheered by the presentation of the necklace, but Zara's swipe at Betty had deflated him. His gasp was exhaustive. He slid to his feet and rushed away. I saw him come to grips with the Rajah.

I knew and he knew that about seventy-five percent of his publicity had gone down the drain with that crack on the face.

"Sid's trying to fix things up," I said to Vicky.

"Do you think Betty will be upset about the slap?" Vicky asked with a happy grin.

Betty was more than upset. She was boiling, she steamed, was getting hotter by the minute, was red hot. A few drops of water cast on her hide at the moment would have been clouds of steam.

Sid came ambling back. Zara rushed toward him and I

was prepared for an explosion, braced my feet to take up the shock, but Zara fooled us. So did Betty, for she did absolutely nothing; but how she seemed to ache to get her hands on Zara's throat! There was murder in her eyes. Zara put a caressing hand about the gob of fat Sid called a neck and cooed, "Aren't they gorgeous, Sid? I'm going to have them appraised at Brock's."

She pulled back her dress and heaved her chest up a bit. The pink pearls rolled.

"You mean the pearls?" I said naively.

She ignored me. "What do you think they're worth, Sid?"

The poor chap was very unhappy, and wiped the perspiration from his brow with a white silk handkerchief.

"I don't know. Anyhow I wouldn't have them appraised, Zara. That wouldn't be nice, would it, Dean?"

"No, most definitely not," I agreed.

She tossed her head. "Don't be silly. You were a darling to arrange this party for me, Sid. I'll never forget it."

Sid was uncomfortable, seemed to be fencing for time. His eyes took on a relieved expression as the Rajah bore down on us. He raised a hand imperiously toward the orchestra. The music stopped instantly just as it had done before. The Rajah bowed and then asked Zara to sing "Harem Scarem Moon"—the theme song of *Blue Lagoon.*

She wasn't even decently bashful about it, had no modesty at all. She was right ready to go ahead, pleased with herself and him too. Some men lifted her to a table and the orchestra played the first pulsating bars of the song.

I heard Sid say to the Rajah, "Just as soon as she finishes."

The Rajah nodded.

I'll say this for Art Rossofif, the fellow who wrote the song—he'd certainly done one swell job with it, there was plenty of zilch, zowie and beat in it.

Zara had one of those lazy, husky, seductive voices that sort of creep right through you. She put the song over beautifully and was encored several times. She loved it.

The Rajah handed her a glass of bubbling champagne. She held up one small hand for silence, then raised her glass and gave a toast.

"To my friends—to my enemies—and to death!"

It was a chilling toast, so unexpected and so defiant.

She tilted her glass and drained it, then burst into wild laughter, almost hysterical, I thought. She hurled the glass into the darkness. A moment later it tinkled into nothingness. Everyone gasped for a full moment, then joined in with her laughter. I found Naomi at my elbow. She turned to me and said, "She makes me sick—always trying to do the unusual. Her every move is planned—she's just a publicity hound."

I said, "You're just sore at her—not that I blame you at all but you must admit the gal knows her stuff."

Naomi sniffed. Then she said a surprising thing for her.

"Most of the men on board have sampled it too," she said.

"Is that nice?" Vicky managed to get her two cents in.

"I really couldn't say—you might ask Dean."

With that parting shot Naomi walked away.

Vicky looked at me and stroked an imaginary chin whisker.

"Young man, is this true? Have you been dilly-dallying with Zara's tiara?"

I buried my head on her bosom and cried brokenly, "Alas! I am undone. 'Twas a balmy summer night, the elephants were roosting in the biscuit bushes—the Whamdoodle was calling to her mate. I was just trying to get the lay of the land."

"Exactly what I was afraid of," she interrupted. "Quit being a fool and sit up."

I told her I'd much rather pillow my head on her

bosom and tell my sad story.

She said, "That's too bad. But you'll have to stay off my hope chest—your beard prickles."

"That's your fault for not warning me about the party," I accused.

Further conversation was interrupted—the Rajah was on the air again. He held up his hand for silence.

"Some excitement for those of you who are interested in swimming. The lovely Zara, as you know, is an excellent swimmer, as are many of you present. To those of you who wish to participate, I will give fifteen minutes to allow you to change—then I shall throw a handful of rubies into the water—they will belong to whoever gets them. The competition is keen but you are all welcome."

"How are we going to see?" someone cried.

"We have provided for that," he replied.

The announcement was greeted with a round of applause, and a general scurrying followed as guests headed for their cabins to change into bathing suits.

"Want a ruby?" I asked Vicky.

"I prefer diamonds," she replied and snuggled close.

"Want to swim?"

"It's too cold. Why don't you go?" she suggested.

"I'd rather be with you. What's a ruby to me?"

"It's nice here," she said.

It was, until an intruder broke the spell.

Sid was at my elbow. He was beaming.

"Well! Am I good or am I good?" he asked anxiously, his smile fading with his question.

I patted him on the back.

"You're terrific," I told him. "Nobody but a Tricker could revive an old chestnut like this and get away with it. What's the Rajah going to sling into the drink—glass beads?"

He held a stubby finger to his lips. "Shush, Dean! Not so loud. Sure—you think I'm crazy, just because I pay you a big salary?"

I nodded. "It's an axiom."

"What's that?" He looked puzzled.

"An axiom's a self-evident truth, but skip it."

I gave the rope a jerk and moved off with Vicky.

"I want to see," she objected.

"So do I—why, I don't know, because it's so phoney. Maybe I want to feel superior to the poor suckers who have fallen for that bewhiskered gag. They're going to be cold and wet for nothing."

Sid stayed with us. "Do you think you can help me fix Betty?" he asked.

I didn't want to tell him then just how low my Betty stock was. "We can try," I promised with no relish for the job. "You ought to do something about Zara. It's a good thing you're not married to that little hell-cat. But things being what they are, I'd take a trip if I were you, Sid. Some safe place, if you can find one in this war-torn world, maybe the South Pole with Byrd."

Sid actually wilted, his face turned a sickly gray. He toddled off. I felt sorry for him—he was a good little guy and I hated to see him taken over the bumps by a frill like Zara—especially when he had an option on my next two novels.

Vicky and I sat down to wait for the show. I gazed longingly at the riding lights of the *Parrakeet* and wished fervently that the party was over and I was back amid Lee Wing, peace and comfort. Shang didn't seem to be happy either. He waddled along, climbed up into my lap and settled down.

The orchestra continued to play, a few people danced, I dozed waiting for the operations to begin.

I heard a laugh—it had a cold, hard ring to it. It was Zara dimly outlined; the Japanese lanterns had been turned off. She was giving the berry to a short, oddly shaped little man. I saw some light through his legs and recognized him at once. It was Zamper. He didn't like her laughter. He caught hold of her wrist. She cried out sharply. Sarakov loomed up to tower over them both. Zamper trotted away.

"That Zamper is an awful-looking runt," Vicky offered. Things were happening. Naomi Ravelle was facing Zara. She came out of the shadows. I don't know what she said but I saw Zara's arm swing up and heard the slap as she struck Naomi across the face. She was the slappingest woman I had seen for some time. Naomi's reactions were quick. She staggered back a moment, then sprang like a tigress. I was looking forward to, expected a fight with no holds barred when Sarakov intervened again, and just in rime. Zara would have been no match for Naomi. The deck was suddenly flooded with lights.

They were all in bathing suits. Naomi in a one-piece yellow outfit and one of those marcelled bathing bathing caps of the same color. Sarakov was a great hulk of a man, all muscles, seemingly made of iron.

Zara was something else. She walked into a spotlight like a moth going to a flame. She shed her anger as quickly and as easily as she cast off her robe. She was all glamour standing there—and I mean all.

I thought at first that she'd forgotten her bathing suit, but when she turned toward us again I saw that she wore a loose-fitting flesh-colored silk handkerchief top, with trunks and bathing cap to match. If you didn't know her psychology of life you would probably have thought her the most ravishingly divine creature in the world. She looked like a pagan goddess. Pagan she was and primitive.

She created a sensation, all right. Even I looked twice. If her costume had been less sensational, my curiosity less pronounced, I might have seen something very important during those few seconds. That is, someone might have seen. As it was we were all busy looking at her, which was what she wanted, and the opportunity passed.

Another searchlight from the bridge flashed on, swept over the deck outlining us clearly for a moment, flashed toward the mystery of the rocky shore and then settled on the water about twenty feet from the hull. I saw a

yellowtail swim past and several barracuda cut the
water, big ones—at least a yard long. I shivered at the
sight of those long lean fish with such cruel jaws. I was in
Florida once when a man was attacked by an Atlantic
barracuda—they are much larger and more ferocious.

We clung to the rail for a front-line view of the show.

To the accompaniment of heavy breathing from some
of the men Zara joined the group in the bow. The
swimmers or rather divers climbed over the rail and stood
poised ready for the dive—hands clutching the rail for
support on that precarious perch.

The water was as calm as the proverbial millpond. It
was low tide and the white sandy bottom showed up
clearly in the moonlight about fifteen feet below the
surface. The swimmers were lined up. First, and nearest
the bow was Zara; then came Naomi; Zamper, the rug
peddler; Michael Sarakov and Basil St. Denis. The others
were strung out; even Betty Potter was going to make a
go at a Woolworth ruby.

The Rajah pushed in next to me, opened the thong
that tied the neck of a chamois bag and cascaded a
shower of glistening red lights into the palm of his hand.
It was like a rain of blood.

"When I count three," he announced, "I will throw the
rubies into the water."

"One—two—three!"

It was fun; exciting too. The rubies glistened in the
bright light, they became little dots floating through the
air to disappear in the water. Instantly fountains of
sparkling water sprang up as the swimmers struck the
surface sending up individual columns before vanishing
beneath the bubbling, churning foam.

We craned our necks to see what was going on. Sid
went in from the ladder with a perfect belly-whopper. At
first we couldn't see much, but after the foam had cleared
away we could make out forms swimming around near
the bottom. Just off the bow the moon reflection created a
blind spot into which some of the swirling bodies

disappeared.

A swimmer broke the surface, it was St. Denis—he took a deep breath and went under again. The short bow-legged Zamper appeared and shouted that he'd got some of the rubies, and swam over to the ladder. Naomi came next, followed a moment later by the big Russian, Sarakov.

I looked around for Zara but couldn't see her anywhere.

A head bobbed up—it was St. Denis. I knew that Zara was supposed to be an expert swimmer, but she should have come up for air before this. Then I thought that she had probably swum around to the other side of the yacht to throw a scare into us and grab off some more sensations.

Suddenly I saw her—just on the near side of the blind spot. She seemed to be suspended a few feet below the surface of the water. She seemed to hang there stiffly without movement. I held my breath expecting her to kick out, to float up, do something. She didn't move. I didn't like it. Something was terribly wrong. I yelled to the big Russian.

"HEY! SARAKOV! SOMETHING'S HAPPENED TO ZARA! SHE'S DOWN THERE!" I pointed to the water as he looked up.

He hung balanced for a minute and then his long body arched into the water. He churned it into a wild milkiness as he swam to the spot I had indicated and then plunged under.

We were all excited. I forgot that I was still tied to Vicky, stepped out of my slippers and leaped overboard. I brought up halfway to the water—cracking my tail smartly against the ship's side. A large form dropped past me into the water. It was Henry Grey. I saw Frank Lane dive in too and Zamper went back. They were all there milling about, being no real help to Sarakov.

I had a ringside seat suspended as I was halfway down the side of the ship. Sarakov came up. He had Zara.

She was limp. Hands were stretched out to aid him as he moved toward the steps.

The excitement had been so intense that I had not noticed the cutting of the rope about my waist until suddenly when I moved I felt I was going to be cut in two and rescued in two pieces. I swung myself around and had some thought of using the rope and walking up the side. Then I remembered Vicky.

I heard someone screaming above me and looked up into Vicky's face from which large tears were streaming. I didn't know she loved me as much as that. I began to feel dizzy. I saw the Rajah's face appear beside Vicky's. Then his body was jerked back. I felt a tug on the rope, knew it was all right and began to help myself. They hauled on the rope until I could get a grip on the rail and sprawl onto the deck.

As I crawled to my feet Vicky put her arms about my neck. She held something in her hand which scratched my face—it was the remains of an evening-dress collar and white tie. I glanced at the Rajah; he'd lost his. Vicky must have pulled on him as he hauled on the rope. She had been determined to save me. If she felt that way about me why didn't she marry me? It was a fleeting thought as we started for the head of the ladder. I was brought up short again —our rope was fouled around a cleat on the deck, which explained why Vicky didn't have her lovely little waist yanked in half when I tossed my carcass over the rail. I cleared the rope. We joined the crowd at the head of the ladder.

Michael Sarakov came first with the limp form of Zara slung over his powerful shoulders. He presented a rather awesome spectacle with the water streaming off him, face distorted with grief, and eyes staring into space straight in front. He strode down the deck with his pathetic burden, barged into the lounge and laid her face down on a cushioned settee. The man was beside himself with grief. Tears were trickling down his cheeks as he straddled the body and commenced artificial respiration tactics. He was counting carefully, his rhythm was perfect.

I bent down to pull out her tongue to help drain the water out of her lungs. One glance at the puffed, distorted features told me the whole story—she was past human aid. I had spent a good many years of my life on the water and consequently had seen a few victims of drowning. But this case was unusual. She could not have been submerged more than a few minutes—three at the most. Her face should not have become so badly swollen in such a short time. I straightened up.

I was about to shake the Russian by the shoulder and tell him it was no use when I saw something on the girl's left leg. It was a long gash under the calf. It was a mean, open cut, bleeding a little, or rather the water and blood oozed out of it. The leg was swollen and turning black. I stood up and looked at the crowd. Sid Tricker, perspiration standing out on his forehead, was tearing at what little hair he had. Henry Grey, pale and haggard, stood beside him. Zamper was biting his nails as he watched Sarakov's futile efforts. Naomi was staring dry-eyed at St. Denis, whose face was a sickly green.

Betty Potter was blubbering on Sid's shoulder—and I suspected her. She believes in getting close to the big shots when they are in trouble. It often paid dividends later. Maybe I'm too cynical. Anyway, she let out a screech when Sid pulled some of her hair by mistake. Our collarless Rajah, his turban cock-eyed, gaped, slack-mouthed and pop-eyed at the body.

To crown it all, Vicky had wrapped her arms around my neck and was sobbing on my shoulder-blade. Altogether it was just about as lousy a windup for a party as one could wish.

I disentangled Vicky's arms from around my neck and shook the big Russian by the shoulder. At first he didn't seem to notice me—finally he turned his head and scowled.

He continued his rhythmic movements, counting,

pressing, releasing.

"It's no use, old man," I said. "She's dead."

He didn't want to believe me. He shook himself. I saw two of the alleged rubies drop to the floor. Sarakov had evidently captured two of them before the tragedy. They sparkled at our feet. He looked at me as if I had taken his breath away.

"It's true," I added. "She was murdered!"

CHAPTER THREE

FOR A MOMENT after my announcement I thought Sarakov was going to leap at my throat. He was enraged first, then bewildered. His eyes were pathetic as he turned them on me. His shoulders sagged, he rose wearily from her body, stepped back a little as I moved forward.

I bent down and turned the body just a little to get a better view of the cut and the rapidly swelling leg.

I heard a gasp. It was the Rajah and he seemed to stagger backward. There were words on his lips which he did not speak. Perhaps he had realized, as I did, the truth about the cut. At least it seemed like a truth then. The cut was under the calf. Zara had dived into the water cleanly and had swum for the bottom; her eyes would have been on the sand below. How, then, did she get that cut on the back of her leg? I knew that there might be broken glass, old tins, or a lost anchor down there, any one of which might have caused the cut if she had been on her back. The cut was quite clean, which meant that it did not come from jagged tin or rusted iron. It must have been from glass, but how? I was puzzled.

The others seemed to have some respect for my inspection or perhaps it was just the natural awe inspired by sudden death. Anyhow they did not crowd me.

I heard someone say hysterically, "She drank to death and was the first one to die."

Sarakov began to cry—horribly and unashamed.

Poor Zara! His were the only tears for her. She looked very tiny and pathetic lying there, not at all like the little firebrand of such a short time before. Her beautiful face was puffed and distorted, her lovely golden body—and it was lovely—was swelling and turning dark. She had lost her handkerchief top in her struggles. Her breasts were hard and round. There were some deep scratches on the right one. I thought then that she must have made the marks with her nails when she tore her upper garment in her fight for air.

Sarakov became calmer. He stood staring dumbly down at her—his huge chest heaving with great sobs. I found myself thinking what a hell of a thing death was. One moment this beautiful golden girl, so vibrantly alive, had been dancing about the decks full of life—the toast of Hollywood. A few minutes later— lying there like a dead fish, meaningless.

A steward came and had the good sense to cover her with a sheet. Together we spread it over the body in a long straight fold.

As I dropped the end over the face I noticed that the dead girl's lips formed a risus sardonicus. I gasped. I hadn't thought of that—the grin of death, a sure sign that poison had been used. Zara had not drowned, she had been poisoned, the cut which had so intrigued me was probably incidental—or was it? How had she been poisoned? What had she taken? When had it been given to her? Was it in the champagne with which she toasted death? How had the murderer been able to time it so perfectly?

I had a queer sensation at the pit of my stomach. Murder! I'd been writing about murder for a long time but that was my first actual contact with a crime. I didn't like it.

"Where's Sid?" I demanded.

He was right at my elbow. "I'm here, Dean," he answered softly.

"Send someone ashore to notify the Avalon police and the coroner. Zara has been murdered!"

Murder!

I heard the word tossed about behind us from lip to lip. There was a murmur which rose and fell and then an interruption; the pest of a Potter stuck her oar in and asked, "Are you sure, Dean? You wouldn't want to make a mistake. You know, just because you're writing about murder doesn't make you an authority, or does it?"

I could have slapped her down but I said, "Do as I tell you, Sid. It's murder. The quicker you notify the police the better it will be for us all."

"Murder!" he cried. "My God, Dean! Do you want to ruin me? Murder! Police! You're crazy. It was an accident! We can bring her around. Try again. Wait," he begged. "Try some more first aid."

I shook my head. "Sorry, Sid. I wish it was only an accident. She's as dead as she'll ever be and she didn't drown, not entirely. Her body bears every symptom of poisoning. It's no accident. This—is murder!"

"Why didn't her body come up?" I heard someone asking behind me. "I thought drowning people always came up at least three times and cried for help."

Funny the ideas people have. Great is the American credo.

Sid was crumpled, seemed to shrink. After a moment or so he called a steward and gave him instructions.

The crowd eased away from the body as if it suddenly had become plague-stricken. I saw fear mount I saw eyes become guarded. I saw people asking themselves if they might be accused.

The steward had not moved. I told him to step on it. He seemed to jerk alive and left the lounge on the run. The crowd started oozing toward the deck. Sid grabbed me by the arm. His face was gray.

"Listen, Dean—say you're only kidding!" he implored. "Tell me the truth, please. This is some gag you cooked up with Zara, the product of your imagination." He raved on, hoping, refusing to face the fact. I shook my head. Some of the people were starting to hurry outside.

"Just a minute, everybody. I think it'd be best if nobody tries to leave the yacht for the present—it might look bad."

Sid let go of my arm and walked dejectedly away. I turned to Vicky, she'd stopped crying, and said, "How about a drink?"

I needed one, knew it would help us both. I was badly
shaken and deeply puzzled. She needed something to
buck her up.

She nodded, we pushed off for the bar.

The place was crowded—everyone had had the same
idea and was busy drinking and talking in whispers.
There was a sudden lull as we entered. I grabbed two
highballs and gave one to Vicky. Sid was a few feet away
with his nose sunk in a long green glass.

I was tempted to wise-crack but didn't. Poor devil, I
was sorry for him again. I put an arm across his shoulder.

"Sorry," I said.

He had been crying. His eyes were wet, there were
tears on his cheeks. He turned his back to me for a
moment. I saw his hand steal up and wipe the tears
away. I took Vicky by the arm and led her to a settee on
deck.

"Who did it?" she demanded.

I shrugged helplessly.

"I thought you knew all about these things," she said.

"Only when they are my own manufacture," I replied.

"Then you're a phoney," she accused.

"A phoney?"

"Yes. You write murder stories and you know nothing
about how to solve a mystery. You drink like a fish and
don't know how to stop, you give me the idea you're in
love with me and . . ."

The poor kid was all mixed up. "And what, Vicky?"

"I don't know. I don't know anything except I feel sure
you'd rather have your booze than anything else."

"Do you like me, Vicky, like me at all?" I asked,
sobered by her remarks.

"I'm tied to you, what more do you want?" she asked
with a suggestion of her old glibness.

"I'm serious, Vicky. I drink but don't usually get
drunk. You've seen me at my worst and at my best. I
know I'm cynical, life has made me that way. I'm in love
with you, love you just as you are. Here's the thing I'm

getting at," I hurried on as she looked up at me, "if you like me now, why do you want to change me, why do you want me to quit drinking, why do you want to make me over? I wouldn't be the same. I might ease up on the drinks for you, to please you. I might even solve this mystery just to prove to you that I'm not a phoney, but why do you want me to do these things?"

She looked at me for a long time. "You're pretty nice as is. If you want to stay that way stick to your writing and remember your name is Mallory and not Sherlock Holmes."

"It's a bargain," I agreed.

As if writing *finis* to the conversation the moon was blotted out by what I thought was a cloud. Anyhow it was dark and I kissed her.

For a while we just sipped our highballs in silence. The more I thought about things the more complicated they became. I was fairly well satisfied in my mind that at least a few people would breathe more easily now that Zara was no longer among us. According to the Hollywood grapevine gossip, the lady had been somewhat of an all-round athlete and hadn't cared much how she accomplished her end so long as she got there. Not that this source of information was worth much; still it usually carried a few grains of truth. It looked as if Sid's pet publicity stunt was turning into one hell of a sticky mess and with plenty of publicity but not the kind he wanted.

Vicky broke into my meditations.

"I s'pose you'll get mixed up in this—show them the master-mind at work?"

I said, "Probably," and patted her on the back. "I'm not going to strain myself but, precious, the sooner this damn thing is solved, the sooner I can get back to the *Parrakeet* and shave so that I can lay my head on your bosom without scraping off any of your lovely hide."

"If that's all that's worrying you, you could possibly, with the aid of your master-mind, find a razor on board the yacht. Betty Potter has one I'm sure," she suggested.

I rumpled her hair. It was blue-black and thick, the sort that's fun to romp around in—and said, "You're quite right, Watson, but I'm particular whose scraper I use— remember? I'm clean from Hollywood and want to stay that way."

"How would you go about solving this?" she asked

"I don't know, Vicky. No one can do anything until the coroner comes."

"What do you think?"

"I have no ideas. There will probably be many suspects. One thing leads to another in a case like this. The row at Ciro's last night probably has some bearing on the case, but I couldn't make a definite statement or even a good guess now. We've seen a lot tonight ourselves and while the things seem slim in themselves they make for clues and suspects."

"Like what?" she demanded.

"Well, we know that Grey and Sarakov had a row about Zara. We saw Sarakov watching them dance. By the way, have you seen a man with a black eye?"

"That was Grey, if you mean the fellow who reeled past us earlier in the evening," she reminded me.

"Right."

"Tell me more," she said.

"We know that Zara slapped Betty and took a poke at Naomi. We don't know why it was done, however, and that's important. We know that Zamper, the rug peddler, was angry with her, grabbed her wrist so that she cried out in pain just before Sarakov arrived on the scene. We know that she has the part which Naomi wanted to play in *Blue Lagoon*."

"I don't think Naomi is the killing kind," she protested.

"Neither do I. I'm just going over the possibilities. There's Sid and there's Frank Lane and, just to make it more complicated, there are all the people on this boat. Any one of them may have wanted to kill her. We've got to find the person, the motive and the opportunity."

"Maybe one of the swimmers held her down," she suggested.

"It's a thought," I agreed. "It's possible, but it couldn't have been for long because the water cleared so rapidly. I didn't look at her throat but I will." Then I remembered. "It's no use, Vicky; she was poisoned."

"How did the murderer—" Her voice trailed off.

"I'm going to have a look at her now. I've thought of something." I started to untie the rope which still bound us.

"Don't, Dean. I feel safer near you." She put her arm in mine and we started toward the lounge and the body of Zara.

The door was closed. I turned the knob but the door would not open. I supposed it had stuck and shoved hard but it did not budge. I ran quickly to the window. I had to peer under the edge of the blind, which had not been drawn completely down. There was only one light burning in the room. Her body was just as we had left it, except for the sheet, which had been disarranged. As I looked into the window I had the feeling that the room was just somehow settling back to normal, that it had been disturbed, that a person had left it hurriedly.

"How can we get in there?" I asked.

"From the bar or through here," she replied and led me toward a door.

We were too late to catch anyone. "I really shouldn't be doing this," I warned Vicky, "but I have a hunch. I stretched the sheet its full length when I put it over her with the steward's help. It was straight and orderly. It is messy and hung in diagonal folds now. Someone probably has my idea."

"What is it?"

"That wound on her leg." I bent closer. "Don't look," I warned.

I took a clean handkerchief from my robe and ran the fold along the open part of the cut. I don't know what I expected to find but certainly not tar. At least I accepted it as tar at the moment.

"Someone's coming!" Vicky whispered.

I drew the sheet back and hurried toward the locked door. We slipped out on deck. I immediately went to the window. Sarakov and the Rajah entered the lounge through the other door. Sarakov knelt down, made the sign of the cross and prayed. The Rajah stood looking down at him.

"So what did you expect to find in the wound?" she asked.

"I hoped the poison. It was a foolish idea, because most stuff is soluble in water or at least would have been washed away. How do you suppose tar got near that cut?" I asked.

"Tar?" she repeated.

"Yes. There's always tar about a boat but I haven't seen any. Of course there could have been some floating in the water. Some may have floated over here from El Segundo where they empty their bilge. I wish the police would come. I'd like to see them get going."

"I thought you were going to solve the case," she teased.

"Not if I can help it. It also depends on the police and how friendly they may be," I reminded her.

Tar! The thought was as sticky as the substance itself. It plagued me, was a challenge, but at the moment my mind was a blank. I was groping for something which eluded me and I kept thinking of tar.

CHAPTER FOUR

FROM THE SHORE came the sound of an outboard motor breaking into life. Presently we made out the dinghy returning. I glanced at my watch—it was eleven-thirty. The boat bumped against the side of the yacht, was made fast and the men ascended the gangway. Sid met them nervously. There was some hand-shaking, then they started for the lounge. Sid called for me.

"Here!" I shouted.

"Come with us," he called.

"Okay!" I took Vicky by the arm and followed the men.

"Took a lot of coaxing to get you—didn't it?" she said.

I told her to be a nice girl and keep quiet.

We caught up with them at the entrance to the lounge. We pushed our way through the gaping crowd at the door. Sid introduced us. One was the captain of the yacht, a short, ruddy-faced man in his early fifties named Red Haslip. Another was a Doctor Wallace, a cadaverous-looking, dead-panned fellow. He wasn't the coroner, the nearest one being on the Mainland, but the deputy sheriff had brought him along. The deputy was a big bruiser, one of those men who fill the eye, large in every way, even in soul, which seems to shine from their eyes. He was young, in his early twenties and likable.

They looked us over for a minute, seemed a little startled at the sight of me and my trailer. The doctor and the deputy exchanged glances—as much as to say the picture crowd were screwy anyway.

The doctor took his little black satchel and went to the body. The deputy—Rocky Stonehead by name—stuck out his granite jaw and asked, "Who decided this was murder?"

Sid was anxious, worried.

"I did," I replied.

"What made you so sure of it?" he asked. "I suppose you know who did it too?"

"No. I've no idea," I answered, wondering if he was going to be hard to handle.

"But you're sure it was murder?" he insisted. "How could you tell if she died in the water?"

"I think you will find that the doctor will agree with me," I answered. "The body shows distinct symptoms of poison. *The risus sardonicus* isn't caused by drowning."

"The what?" he asked.

"*Risus sardonicus*," I repeated and then explained, "The grin of death."

"Well, let's take a look." He walked to the couch, we followed.

Sarakov and the Rajah were standing in the background.

Rocky stood beside the doctor. "She must have been a swell looker," he mused then. "What do you make of it, Doc?"

The doctor bent down, raised one of Zara's eyelids and flashed a small lamp on it. Next he sniffed at her mouth, then straightened up and pursed his lips thoughtfully. He examined the scratches on the right breast a moment, considered them, and finally removed the sheet and dropped it to the floor.

He made funny little sounds as he examined the cut on her leg. He took a small swab from his satchel and probed through the wound, then withdrew it. I wondered what he would find and clutched the handkerchief in my pocket. The cotton came out discolored with clots of blood and some small particles of the same sticky black substance that I had found. He pulled out and used a small magnifying-glass to examine the swab.

'Tar!" he muttered.

"You mean she was poisoned with tar?" Rocky asked.

I turned to look at Sarakov, who was standing just inside the door with his arms folded across his chest. He was gazing straight ahead, seeing nothing, seemingly hearing nothing.

"Er—no," the doctor mumbled. "There are signs of poison, no doubt of that. Death was induced probably by a combination of both. Offhand I'd say that the poison was undoubtedly strong enough to have killed her without the drowning factor. There is some trace of water in her lungs, however. It's impossible to say what kind of poison was used or how it was administered until an autopsy has been performed. The only tangible thing is this black substance that I have taken from the wound. It doesn't smell like tar, but it looks like it. I'll have it analyzed."

I stepped forward. "Mind if I take a look at it, Doc?"

He turned a pair of watery blue eyes on me and seemed about to refuse, thought better of it, shrugged an agreement. I took the glass from his fingers and bent over the swab. I returned the glass and thanked him.

"Well," Rocky inquired, "know what it is?"

"No."

Sarakov turned and went softly from the room

Sid cut in then. "Mr. Mallory is a well-known writer of mystery stories; he knows all about murder, poisons and things like this."

"Oh," Rocky said and I didn't like the inflection of his voice.

I don't believe Sid had any intention of getting me in wrong but he certainly planted the germ of suspicion in Rocky's head with those remarks of his.

"What's next, Doc?" Rocky asked.

"I think we should remove the body, or would you rather it remained here?" he asked.

Rocky shrugged.

"Isn't there a mortuary in Avalon?" I asked. "It would probably be better there," I suggested.

"You're in charge, Stonehead. It's up to you to decide," the doctor prompted.

"May as well take her ashore," Rocky agreed.

A stretcher was brought in. Sarakov came with the men, brushed them aside and lifted Zara from the couch and placed her gently on the canvas. He covered her with a sheet, then stepped back. "Be careful," he warned.

The doctor collected his instruments. "You'd better start a preliminary investigation," he suggested as he followed the men and the stretcher.

Rocky ran a hand through his shock of bushy hair. "I'm no detective," he growled. "I'm just a summer deputy hired to keep the boys and girls in order on the beaches and around the harbor at night."

Vicky gave me a poke in the ribs. "It's your chance, Hawkshaw," she whispered.

"Better not let anyone leave this boat," the doctor cautioned from the door.

Rocky looked at us long and steadily. There was grim purpose in those eyes of his. "Well," he said, "I size it up this way. This fellow and the Doc have agreed that she was poisoned. You all know what that means. Has anyone left the boat since it happened?" he demanded.

We were all prompt with our denials.

"Then nobody goes," he declared. "Remember that," he warned.

"What are you going to do?" Sid asked.

"Look, mister, I'm no regular dick. I've already told you that. The Chief's on a fishing trip down to the islands and won't be back until morning. In the meantime, until the Chief arrives, or they send someone over from the Mainland, I'll stand guard." He patted his bulging hip meaningly. "Nobody gets away from this boat, understand?"

That meant that we were sunk indefinitely.

Rocky went to the door and exclaimed, "We're in for it now!"

I followed him, realized at once what he meant. The cloud which I had seen obscure the moon was a fog bank which had moved in and had us completely enveloped. The yacht was shrouded in ghostlike mist. The rigging seemed damp and lifeless in the still air. The lights on the shore were fading fast.

"It's thick," I heard the doctor's voice come up from below. "Better hurry so we'll know where we're going."

Rocky stepped out and leaned over the rail. He shouted, "Call the Mainland again, will you, Doc? Get them to send someone over here. I'll stand guard, but one man alone with this crowd hasn't much of a chance."

"Okay," floated back to us. Then the rapid roar of a motor sounded. We could hear the bubble and churn of the water, saw the boat for a moment as she slipped away.

"Well, that's that," Rocky said and turned around.

He eyed me for a moment. "You seem pretty interested in the things that go on," he said.

"Naturally. I've written about murders for years but never came in contact with one before."

"You've got nothing on me. I'm not even a—" He stopped. "Who discovered the murder?" he asked.

"I believe I did," I replied.

"Don't you know?"

"I didn't know she was dead at the time. We were on deck, Miss Blaire and myself, when I realized that all was not well with Zara."

"How do you suppose she came by that cut on her leg? It doesn't look like a cut she'd get from anything on the bottom."

I grabbed at his arm. "That cut!" I cried. "That's probably the answer! I've been trying to put the pieces of the puzzle together ever since—" I stopped. I very nearly told him about my probing of the wound.

"Ever since what?" he asked.

"The doctor probed the wound and called the black stuff tar. I've been trying to remember. You see, in my writing I must know many things about poisons and other things. I think now I have the answer."

"You mean you know the poison?" he asked.

My head was moving up and down slowly as I began to assure myself that I was on the right track.

"What is it?" Vicky asked eagerly.

"Sure, let me in on it too," Rocky urged.

I paused to light a cigarette.

"Years ago, so long ago that I had forgotten about it," I began, "long before I became a writer of alleged mystery stories—I wrote an adventure novel. It was called *Curare*. The locale was the headwaters of the Orinoco River. The natives in that part of the world use a poison on their arrows. If taken internally the poison will cause little or no harm, but if it gets in the blood-stream—it's deadly. It acts rapidly, first attacking the power of speech, next the arms and respiratory organs. In its natural state it is a black resinous substance, that comes from a Strychnos shrub, very similar to what you saw on the swab. In its refined alkaloid form, it becomes a yellow powder, known here as curarine, and is used in small doses for the purpose of vivisection. Offhand I'd say the knife was poisoned, was probably a knife with a groove or a ridge that would hold the curare. Zara had the symptoms of a curare victim. Now all you have to do, Mr.—er—Stonehead, is to find the knife."

"As simple as that," he said. "Who had a knife? Did you see one?"

"No."

"So we start searching this tub," he said. "Is that it?"

The thing I call a brain began to work. "Listen, officer," I said. "You look like a good egg, so I'm going to give you a tip."

"What?" he asked flatly.

I heard a few dull blasts of fog-horns, hoarse voices caught in the fog—complaining voices. Then there was something else, louder and more insistent, the sound of a plane. We all looked up but could see nothing through the milkiness which surrounded us.

"Sounds like one of the hydroplanes from the Mainland," he said, his face lighting up. "Just my luck that they can't land."

The drone of the motors grew louder, faded, came louder again, sputtered angrily and then buzzed away.

"They've gone back," he said with disappointment. "Probably the police too."

"There wouldn't have been time, Stonehead. It was more likely a coast guard plane. Too bad; we could have used them."

"We sure could," he agreed, his face now quite crestfallen.

I put a hand on his shoulder and said, "Do you realize that this is the biggest opportunity of your life?" His eyes opened a bit at this. "This dead girl is Zara. Zara—man, she's known internationally to millions of movie fans. The fellow who solves this murder is going to have his face spread over the front pages of the leading newspapers of the world. And you want to wait until your chief gets back from a fishing trip so that he can grab off all the glory for himself!"

I saw a light dawning in the man's eyes.

"That's so—I never thought of that. But how the hell am I going to solve the murder before he gets back? I don't even know what to do."

"When do you think he will get back—or anyone get over from the Mainland, for that matter?" I asked

"You can't tell about fogs," he sighed.

"Exactly! And while we're held here by this fog you'll have the field to yourself. I'd like to help you, if you'd let me."

He actually smiled and put a big paw on my shoulder.

"Say, that's mighty fine of you. I sized you up as being a right guy from the start. The only trouble is, I'm no man-hunter. I'm just a deputy and murder ain't in my line. I'm a football player working for the summer. I probably know less about murder than you do."

So that was why his face seemed so familiar! Rocky Stonehead! I should have recognized him at once. I shot him a quick glance, because that last statement of his was a perfect rib.

He didn't bat an eye but went on, "I'd be like those dumb lugs you read about in mystery stories. You know, the cop is always dumb."

I knew. I had been guilty of the trick myself and it was exactly what I thought he was and would be. He surprised me. I wanted to have a go at the case. Nature had played into my hands by sending fog and now this man with an awareness of his own limitations was doing the rest.

"Let's get started," I suggested. "I don't want to seem to usurp your prerogative but I've a little something at stake in this case."

"That's all right," he said, "and it's sure swell of you, Mr. Mallory."

"Then we can get going, Mr.—er—Stonehead."

"Look," he said, "if we're going to be together why don't you call me Rocky? My friends do."

"Okay, Rocky, it's a bargain. We work together."

"What do you want to do first?"

"See if we can find the knife," I replied.

"How?"

"We'll need a little cooperation from the captain and a pair of swimming trunks for me."

"Why don't you let me go over? I used to be one of the boys who did his stuff under the glass-bottom boats. You know, dive under, pry abolone shells off the rocks and that sort of thing."

"Fine. We'll need a powerful light. If we take it down to the surface of the water, the fog will act as a reflector and show the bottom very clearly," I explained. "Let's get going."

We saw the captain, got the lamp and the three of us went down the ladder to the landing stage.

"What's your idea?" Rocky asked. He shivered a little, dressed as he was in swim pants, not even a towel over his broad shoulders.

"I've an idea the knife was tossed under the boat, I don't believe it was brought up by the murderer."

"And the tide has begun to turn, so we can't be sure where the boat lay at the time of the murder," he said.

"We're in approximately the same position," the captain's voice called down from above. "When I saw the fog rolling in I put out a stern anchor."

"That's a help," Rocky agreed. "Now if you'll tell me where she was I'll have a try."

We did our best to give him the approximate location of Zara but it was difficult to be exact. He didn't complain, just dove in.

"No wonder he was a life-guard," Vicky said.

I'm fairly well set up myself but in comparison with Rocky I knew I was no Hercules.

Rocky came up, held onto the edge of the landing stage a moment to get his breath and »then slipped down. He was up and down at least half a dozen times. The light glowed on the surface but that did not prevent our seeing him at work. He seemed to do it with such little effort. He had an uncanny underwater sense. He never covered the same ground twice. He was very systematic about it. We could see his head turn from side to side as he swam about like some great fish.

Vicky clutched at my arm. Rocky seemed excited down below. He changed his course, reached for some thing, and came floating up, sending little bubbles ahead of him. He had a knife in his hand. He dropped it on the landing stage and crawled up. He sat there gasping for a few seconds; then rose to his feet.

"I had been looking for something shiny," he said. "The boy who did the trick was a good swimmer and knew his way about underwater. The knife was plunged into the bottom, dug right into the sand. In a day or so it would have been completely covered and probably never found." He shook himself like a great Dane. "It was smart of you to think of the knife," he said.

"And smarter of you to find it half buried as it was," I threw back at him.

I wrapped the knife in the handkerchief I had used when I probed the wound.

"Get into your clothes," Vicky urged.

"It's not a bad idea," he agreed. "Neither was yours, about the light and all."

The captain was at the head of the ladder. "Any luck?" he asked.

I nodded. I didn't want the people on the yacht to know what we had accomplished if I could help it.

"I'll be with you in a minute," Rocky promised and padded away.

"Did anyone watch us?" I asked the captain.

"There were a few curious people at first who wanted to know what you were doing. I told them you were fishing for a watch. They were more interested in the bar."

"Did you know any of them?"

"Yes. Mr. Tricker, Mr. Grey and the Rajah were the ones who were particularly interested."

"That's fine," I said. We thanked him and moved along the deck. I whispered to Vicky, "We have our first clue."

CHAPTER FIVE

ROCKY CAME BACK with a nice healthy glow. We went to the lounge with our prize. I opened the handkerchief and examined the knife. My guess had been right. There was a slight groove along the edge of the blade and in it mixed with sand from the bottom there was enough of the same dark sticky substance to make me feel sure that I was right on all counts up to that moment.

Vicky looked too and exclaimed, "Why, that's just like the knife I bought for my fishing kit!" She reached forward, would have touched it, but I held her hand away.

I left the knife and handkerchief on the table and went to the settee where Zara's body had lain.

I saw something gleaming on one of the cushions. It was one of the fake rubies the Rajah had thrown overboard. It was on the end cushion where her head had lain. She must have found one and put it in her mouth, and it had probably fallen out when the big Russian was giving her artificial respiration.

"What is it?" Rocky asked.

I was too busy thinking to answer his question. If Zara had found one of the baubles, then she had been stabbed by someone, an excellent swimmer, as Rocky suggested, a few seconds after they had entered the water. I tried to think back, to recall what had happened just after they dived. There was an awful splash and that was all I could remember until I was startled by seeing her practically lifeless underneath. It must have been curare that was used. It had to be. That would explain her lifelessness. Curare starts a paralysis almost immediately; that too would explain the water in her lungs. She had had no chance to do anything. When realization had struck her that something was wrong she had probably clutched at her chest while fighting for air, which would explain the scratches on her breast.

Rocky repeated, "What is it?"

"A genuine Woolworth ruby, if I'm not mistaken —one of the handful that the Rajah threw overboard."

"What Rajah?" he asked.

I was explaining the set-up to him when the high-pitched tones of an enraged woman's voice cut across my conversation. We all listened. The door banged open and Betty Potter charged in. Her hair was awry, her clothes rumpled. There was murderous hate in her eyes as they blasted at Rocky.

"I want to go ashore, do you hear?" she shouted.

"I heard you, but nobody goes ashore," he replied stolidly. Betty meant nothing to him, could influence him in no way.

"But you don't understand." She tried some sweet persuasion.

"Look! Mr. Mallory here is my deputy assistant on account of the fog, and he said to keep everybody on board," Rocky explained patiently.

I nodded my approval over her head.

She made a quick turn about to glare at me. "Somebody's going to catch hell for this!" she shrieked. "The biggest scoop I've had in years and you"—her voice was withering with contempt—"won't let me phone it in. Imagine my having to ask you!"

"One never knows, Betty, does one?"

"Oh!" She shot half a ton of exasperation in the one word and stalked away, down the length of the cabin. She seemed to be adjusting her mental attitude for a new attack.

"Who's the battle-ax?" Rocky asked in a stage-whisper.

That naive question upset Betty's new campaign. Betty, as you may have guessed, thought well of herself and knew her power in certain circles. Like so many of us, she forgot the limit of her influence. She blew up again.

"Why, you big, dumb ignorant ox! I'm Betty Potter of the New York *Sphere* and I demand that you allow me to go ashore immediately!"

Rocky grinned, a nice grin, wide, easy, tolerant.

"Lady," he said, "I don't care if you're Cleo out of Egypt, nobody goes ashore until this murder's solved. Ain't that right, Mr. Mallory?"

"Is that so!" she screamed. "Well, I'm going ashore! No half-baked author, deputy or not, is going to keep me here." She turned to Rocky. "Don't you dare to stop me!" She swung on her heels.

Rocky raised his bushy eyebrows. "Oh yeah?" he said and stretched one of his great paws after her, caught her and drew her back.

Betty went into action. Smack! She struck Rocky clean across the rock of his lower jaw. A red spot blurred on his face for a moment. Then he pinned her other arm to her side. He didn't seem to be ruffled even a little bit. What a man!

"Take your dirty hands off me!" she shrilled. She began to kick at his shins.

I moved forward and said, "Now, Betty—don't get your shirt tied in a knot. You have just assaulted an officer in front of witnesses. We could put you under arrest for that, but we won't, not at the moment. Your attitude is unfortunate. Your actions very suspicious. Why this haste to get away? Have you something to hide? You are a probable suspect, you know, or don't you?"

She had been listening and watching filled with incredulity. "Me?" she managed to gasp.

"You did have a set-to with Zara, didn't you?" I demanded.

"But, Dean, you know—why, I'm a newspaper woman. You—"

I winked at Rocky, took Betty by the arm and ushered her toward a door that I'd had my eye on for the last few moments. She favored Rocky with a dirty look as we moved away. I opened the door and bowed her in, saying, "You'd better think it all over." I stepped back, shut and locked the door and said to Rocky, "We'll call that the brig for the moment."

"Hey, you bastard—this is a washroom!" she howled.

I said, "Could be, Betty. Try it."

She pummeled on the heavy door with her fists, crying, "Let me out, you dirty louse!" She waited for a moment while we grinned at each other. "If you don't I'll spill what I know about you and Vicky!" she threatened.

I laughed back at her, stood close to the door and said, "I don't think you will. Have a seat, Betty—meditation is good for the soul."

As I turned away from the door I bumped into Vicky, who had come up to hear La Potter's wails.

"Listen, precious!" I said. "It looks as if I'm going to be busy for some time, so I'm going to untie you. Be a good girl and go to your cabin and take a snooze."

"Nothing doing—it isn't safe for you to be running around loose. What would have happened to you if you hadn't been tied to me when you jumped overboard? Say, you big egg, can you swim?"

I tweaked her little nose and said, "You win, beautiful."

We walked back to Rocky and sat down. He was grinning from ear to ear.

"You're all right," he said, "for a writer. It was swell, the way you got rid of that dame."

She was still screaming and banging at the door but it was faint enough not to be annoying; rather satisfying, in fact.

"I enjoyed it myself—I've been wanting to put her in her place for a long time. Now that the excitement's over for the moment, I may as well give you a rough outline of what's been going on around here prior to the murder. I need a little reviewing myself.

"Zara, the dead girl, was to have played the lead in a picture called—*Blue Lagoon,* a South Sea picture, in which the leads had to be expert swimmers. Sid Tricker, whom you've already met, is president of the company that's going to make the film. Sid's one of the greatest publicity hounds in the business and conceived the brilliant idea of renting this yacht for a publicity stunt to ballyhoo the picture. He hired a fellow from Central Casting to play the part of a phony rajah, who was supposed to own an island at some place called Benang. Most of the cast from the picture are on board, plus our friend Betty Potter who was to do the write-up. Everything went along all right until the rajah announced that he was going to toss a handful of rubies overboard—they were glass like the one I showed you—and finders keepers. A number of guests put on bathing suits, including Zara, and dived in after the alleged rubies.

"Zara was the first to dive. Then Naomi, Zamper, Sarakov and St. Denis. Betty Potter followed; then Henry Grey. They all came up except Zara. I saw her body below the surface and yelled to the big Russian Sarakov. He went under and came up with her. He carried her into the lounge, where it was discovered that she was dead. Then we sent for the police and the doctor. The rest you know."

He pushed his weather-beaten felt hat back and scratched his head.

"Well—I guess it's up to us to start grilling 'em, and judging by the mob that's on board, it'll be a man-sized job. Say—where in hell were they all supposed to bunk?"

Vicky answered, "Most of them had reservations at the hotel; there were only a few of us that had cabins."

"I get you—just the ones that're palsy-walsy with the big shot, eh?"

I nodded.

"Well, what do we do now?" he demanded.

"We'll need a few deputies to help us keep watch. We'd better see the captain, enlist the crew as special deputies. What do you think of that?"

"I did that," he said. "I swore the captain in as a

deputy and made his crew assistants. That's why your friend Betty looked as if she had gone through the mill. She probably tried to get gay with one of the sailors."

"You'll do, Rocky," I approved.

"And how," Vicky added with a little too much fervor, or so it seemed.

I let it pass but made up my mind to take up a course in how to have muscles, you know the kind, in ten easy lessons.

"What's next?" he asked. "Shouldn't we be asking people a lot of questions?"

"That will come. A little later. There's a trick I'd like to do first. Take a look in Zara's cabin. . . . Do you know which one it was?" I asked Vicky.

She shook her head.

"Suppose I ask the little guy—you know, Tricker. I'll let you know," he promised.

"You'll probably find him in the bar," I suggested as he started off.

"I like him," Vicky said.

"I was afraid of that."

"Don't be a goon, Dean. You're tops with me. As a matter of fact I've been worrying about you."

"Why?"

"If you go on with this murder, get involved in its solution, you'll be in the number one spot for danger. It isn't worth it, Dean."

"But you are. You called me a phony, remember, and I said I'd prove that I'm not. Things have played into my hands. It will be great publicity. Imagine having my name splashed across the papers like this: WRITER OF MYSTERY STORIES SOLVES CRIME."

"Aren't you forgetting something? You promised the glory to Rocky," she reminded me.

"So I did. Well, I think publicity is the bunk anyhow."

As we left the lounge she cried, "Poor little Shang— I've lost him!" She began a systematic search of the lounge.

I'd forgotten all about the little tyke. I looked around too. The Peke was among those missing, all right.

"When did you have him last?" I asked anxiously.

"I don't remember—oh, yes, I do. It was just before you went on the knife expedition."

I remembered that part of it. I began to feel blue. I was very fond of the little snorter.

"Someone probably picked him up. He's on the boat somewhere," she said hopefully.

"Then he's in the bar. Let's go."

The bar was crowded. There was a lot of laughter. I guessed why even before Vicky cried, "Shang!"

There he was, the little soak, tanked to the ears. Someone had put him on the bar and true to form he had been tasting drinks. Vicky was angry and barged ahead. Shang, hearing his name, leered at us. She picked him up, glowered at the people who had been laughing at his drunken antics, and came back to me.

Sid had buttonholed me. "Know anything, Dean?" he asked.

"Not a thing, Sid, but we're going to work right now. Where's Rocky? He was looking for you."

"Right here, waiting," Rocky answered from behind me.

He led us to Zara's cabin. The decks were wet and slippery. The night was thick, things showed indistinctly through the fog. A light burned dimly overhead.

"This is it," Rocky said and pointed toward a door. I held out my hand for silence. There were footprints clearly outlined on the deck leading into her cabin. A lamp was glowing inside. Softly we went to the door. Someone was moving about inside.

"Want my gun?" Rocky whispered.

"I hope not," I replied and opened the door.

CHAPTER SIX

THE MAN'S BACK was turned toward us. He was crouched before a wardrobe trunk engaged in a systematic search of the drawers. He did not hear us, did not know we were watching him until Shang said, "Whurrps." He turned, surprised, a guilty look on his face, in his eyes. It was Henry Grey, the president of the Grey Air Lines.

"Hope we're not intruding, but I've been placed in charge of the investigation, so I'm afraid I'll have to ask you to explain what you're doing here," I said.

The man's face was drawn and gray, but he kept his poise admirably.

"Mallory," he said, "I know it looks like the devil. The fact is I'd written a number of letters—rather foolish ones—to Zara. I'm trying to find them. In my position I couldn't very well afford to have the Sunday supplements get hold of them."

"I can sympathize with you—the boys on the tabs would have a swell time with them—but this is a serious business. I'm afraid I'll have to search you."

He shrugged. "Go ahead—I've found nothing. She probably didn't bring them with her. It was a long chance anyway."

He had changed from his oriental costume into white flannels, turtleneck sweater and gray tweed sport jacket. I looked again to see if his eye was going to be black. It was all right, the red welt on his cheek was fading.

I found nothing in his pockets but a pipe, tobacco pouch and some matches.

I didn't believe that gag about letters but I wanted him to think that I did. "If I come across any letters of yours I'll try to keep them out of the case," I promised.

"Thanks, Mallory—awfully decent of you."

He bowed to Vicky and walked out of the cabin.

She put Shang on the floor and sat down on the bed. I looked over the small vanity table. It was massed with bottles of expensive perfumes, powders, cold creams and the usual female accessories used to lead the male to slaughter. I turned from that to the little drawers in the wardrobe trunk—the same one that had interested Grey. The first one contained a flock of stockings. The second some filmy sets of step-ins, brassieres and what have you. The third and last drawer produced a number of letters. I hauled them out for inspection. They were mostly bills for useful amounts from exclusive shops in Westwood and Beverly Hills.

"You don't need me in here, do you?" Rocky asked.

"Not at the moment. Why?"

"I think I'll circulate around a bit. May be able to pick up some information. I'll see you later."

"I'll bet he's going for a drink," Vicky conjectured.

"Don't be like that. Was your father a drunkard, or what?" I asked.

I went back to my hunt and really found something. It was a photograph of a beautiful girl holding a tiny baby in her arms. I handed it to Vicky.

"Know who that is?" I asked.

She looked at it and her eyes opened wide. "Why, that's Naomi—I didn't know that she . . ."

"Neither did I. Not wishing to cast any reflections on the gal's virginity—still you may recall that she disappeared for a few months last year, a trip to her native city, or was it an appendicitis story? She did have an operation, I believe. Anyway we'll keep this—it might be useful."

I rummaged a little farther and came upon a heavy manila envelope—it was sealed. I opened it and got a surprise. It contained a Mexican marriage license dated four months back in Mexicali, certifying that Zara and our publicity seeker, Sid Tricker, had joined hands in holy matrimony. That was news. Leave it to a woman to carry important documents around loose. That was one thing Betty Potter had missed—or had she? A dainty morsel like that could pay interesting dividends if used intelligently. I added it to the photograph in the pocket of my Mandarin robe.

Vicky slipped off the bed and walked into the tiny bathroom. Shang started barking at something. I looked down and found him under the bed yapping at something white on the floor. I got on my hands and knees and reached for it and picked it up. It was a small ball of paper, crumpled in anger and tossed away in the heat of excitement. On it was written in a fine hand, "Unless you bring them with you I shall give out interesting information about Shanghai, Vladivostok and the slave market at Teheran."

It was not signed, but it cleared the air considerably and gave some possible motive for the murder. Someone wanted something or else they would expose Zara's past, which she probably had excellent reasons for wanting kept dark. The writing looked like that of a woman.

"Shanghai, Vladivostok and Teheran," I repeated the names of the three critics.

"You're covering an awful lot of territory," Vicky said.

"So did she, evidently," I replied and handed her the note.

I found a jewel-box, an exquisite thing made of white gold, encrusted with semi-precious stones, sapphires and aquamaraines. I opened it to find it full of ashes. "Damn!" I cried.

"What now?" she asked.

"This box is full of ashes, ashes of paper, and important paper, I'd like to bet."

She came close and poked a finger at the curled bits of paper. They crumbled under her touch. "You shouldn't have done that," I said. "There were marks on it, lines, and I was trying to figure out what they were."

"I'm sorry. I didn't know, and you didn't have to bark at me," she accused.

"Keep your fingers out of things and I won't bark," I shot back. I closed the box and dropped it back on the dressing-table.

I had uncovered some information that I didn't enjoy knowing and that was all the room offered. "Come on, Vicky—there's nothing more we can do here," I said.

I stepped away from the dressing-table and stopped. On the floor there was a small piece of paper, blue paper—and it was charred along one edge. I gave a sigh of relief and bent down to pick it up. I turned back to the dressing-table, opened the box and tried the bit of paper along its edge. It was one corner of the thing that had been burned and it had been a blue-print. It was such a small piece of paper that I was afraid of losing it. I found one of Zara's handkerchiefs which reeked of perfume and dropped the paper into it.

I took Vicky by the arm, tucked Shang under my wing and went out on deck calling for Rocky.

He came in a hurry and seemed excited. "I got some dope," he announced.

I said, "Swell," and kept going toward the lounge.

"I was talking to the cook, and he said one of the stewards told him."

"And why were you talking to the cook?"

"I was chilly and went to the galley to get something warm. This fog gets into your bones. The steward said . . ."

"Skip it," I said; "and while I'm your assistant I insist on your maintaining the dignity of our position —in other words, wipe the chalotte russe off your chin. Now what did the steward tell the cook?"

"She told the bow-legged man she'd see him in hell first, and bow-legs told her to save a good place for him because she'd get there first."

"We'll put that information on ice," I promised.

He grinned sheepishly. Together we went to the lounge. It was empty. I suddenly remembered that Betty Potter was still locked in the washroom. I unlocked the

door and said loudly, "Make way for the Privy-Councilor."
She stalked out—she was mad as the devil. She
glared at the three of us and walked quickly from the
lounge without saying a word, thereby establishing an
all-time record for herself.

I smiled after her, wondering what she would concoct
to pay me back. She'd get back at me, of that I was
certain. Well, there was no point worrying about a sure
thing. I'd know when the time arrived.

"Get Grey," I said.

"Why Grey?" Vicky asked.

"That little piece of paper. I've just decided that the
part of the word on it was 'trons.' I've been trying to fit
pieces together. Grey is the only on man on board who
might be interested in a blue-print. Grey was searching
the cabin; I don't believe the letter story at all. It's a shot
in the dark and worth taking."

"I hope none are fired at you," she said. Then added,
"Rocky is a help. I like the Great Dane. He's nice, and
comfortable and good, but," she added, "he wouldn't be
exciting."

I was digesting that bit of feminine estimation when
Rocky returned with Grey. He came in, quite unruffled,
sat down and proceeded to light his pipe. I wasn't at all
sure that his pose was not too studied.

"Grey," I began, "I wish you'd be good enough to give
me an outline of your acquaintance with Zara—when you
met her, where, and anything else that you think might
be helpful."

He puffed on his pipe a moment, deep in thought,
then started in. "I met her in San Francisco about a year
ago—in a night club."

"The Purple Domino," I suggested because I knew it
was run by a foreign crowd. I had heard stories about it.

"Yes, that's the one. I was very much taken with her,
and for a while I saw a good deal of her. To make a long
story short, a month later I asked her to marry me. She
was evasive and told me that she would think it over. A

week later she went to Hollywood. I did not see her again for some months. A couple of weeks ago I was in Los Angeles on business and looked her up. She seemed very glad to see me again and we had lunch at Perino's. He paused, as if considering something. He jerked his head up suddenly. "I guess I'd better tell you the whole thing." I nodded. "I came to this party at her request. She wired me yesterday asking me to come—also for a loan of ten thousand dollars which she said she would repay in a few weeks."

We seemed to be getting somewhere at last.

"And you brought the money?"

"Yes—but I didn't have a chance to give it to her. We spoke about it when we were dancing together. I was to see her in her cabin later."

"That was a break for you. Did she ever ask you for an amount like that before?"

"Once—shortly after she left San Francisco."

"And you gave it to her?"

"I sent it to her. I could not give it to her in person as I had to leave immediately for Miami on business. We were opening a new passenger route to Rio."

"Did she repay you the loan?"

"No."

My reaction to that was purely feminine. I guess writers and actors, most artists, are intermixed with a dash of instincts of both sexes. I looked across at Vicky and sensed definitely that she felt as I did. Henry Grey was being a frank witness, that is, pretending frankness, but in reality under the guise of telling me all he knew he was concealing important things which he hoped would be undiscovered because of his apparent willingness to talk.

"So, she was a chiseler. Any idea why she needed the money?"

"No—I never asked her."

"That was a lot of money to be handing out without asking what it was needed for—wasn't it?"

He shrugged his wide shoulders.

"I'm a wealthy man and, as I told you, I was in love with Zara."

"And what about the ten thousand dollars?"

He made a wry face.

"I was debating whether or not I should tell you when your man came for me. It may or may not have direct bearing on the case but I think you should know. Someone has stolen the ten thousand dollars."

That was a neat bit of information and carried overtones. Zara was probably being blackmailed. Did the person who wrote the note steal the money? Was that person the murderer? I was inclined to doubt that, as blackmailers are seldom murderers, certainly they don't kill the goose that lays the golden egg.

"Tell me about it," I said.

"It was in my wallet in the desk in my cabin. I put it there when we changed for the diving stunt. Because of the subsequent excitement I forgot all about it until a few minutes ago. When I looked for it, it was gone."

"Have you been out of your cabin much since you changed?"

"Only the time you found me in her cabin, and once to the bar for a drink."

"Do you remember the denominations of the bills?"

"I do—ten one-thousand-dollar bills. I preferred giving her the money in cash rather than use a check or bank draft."

I felt there was some information here if I could get the man to tell the truth.

"Then you were afraid of her, Grey—afraid that she might use a check to compromise you?"

"Not afraid, Mallory—just naturally cautious." Then he added with a half-smile, "You see, I've been around."

"I can't help feeling that you're covering something, Grey, so I'm going to give you some information that may alter the picture for you. Supposing that while you were loaning her money and possibly expecting to marry her, she were already married to someone else—a wealthy man? Would that make any difference in your story?"

He considered this for a moment. "It might—but she hadn't married anyone, so why talk about it?"

"That's where you're wrong, Grey. She did get married in Mexico, six months ago, and to a wealthy man."

Grey plucked at his lower lip thoughtfully.

"Hmm. Well, that does change things a bit."

"I thought it would. Putting it crudely, it amounts to this—the lady in question, while keeping you on the string and getting money from you, was married to another man and getting money from him. At the same time she was carrying on an affair with at least one other man. All of which leads me to believe that she was pretty much of an all around athlete."

The man grinned ruefully.

"That explains a lot, Mallory. Up to now I'd been giving her the benefit of the doubt—that somebody had a hold on her and was forcing her to do things. Now it appears that she had quite a few ideas of her own." He gave a deep sigh. "I suppose you'd like to hear the whole sad story."

I nodded.

He settled himself more comfortably in his chair, filled his pipe, lit it, and leaned back. When it was drawing well he began: "As I told you, I first met her in a night club in San Francisco about a year ago. I'll never forget the first time I saw her. The club had been decorated to represent a jungle. The lights were dimmed and you could hear the faint muttering of tomtoms. Suddenly at a signal, she appeared wearing only a loincloth and commenced swaying to the throbbing drums. Presently the drums became louder and she went into a wild primitive dance. There was something about the gleam of her lovely body and the flashing of her eyes and teeth that held me spellbound.

"Later she sang the *Song of the Island*. You've heard her sing, and heard that strange haunting quality of her voice. I became instantly infatuated. I'd been infatuated before, but had always managed to keep them segregated so that I controlled them. This, however, was different; it left me dazed. To be quite frank —I decided that I had to have her even if it meant marriage. The manager of the club was under an obligation to me, so I could do pretty much as I pleased around there. He took me to her dressing-room and introduced me. The upshot of it all was that she left with me that night. I have a villa on the cliffs at Carmel. We spent a week there."

He paused a moment, sucking quietly on his pipe, his mind awhirl with pictures of that week in Carmel, memories that stirred afresh, like the finding of a rose pressed between the pages of a long-forgotten book. Suddenly he frowned—breaking the spell.

"Sorry," he said, "but in spite of subsequent events, it was the most perfect week of my life."

I could understand that part of it although the lady had never been to my liking. I was quite sure that if she made up her mind to be thoroughly alluring she would do a magnificent job of it. Grey was lucky he didn't end up by bursting into flame.

"Like a fool," he continued, "I thought she was in love with me and—I suppose it was a case of dog in the manger—I asked her to marry me. But she put me off by saying that things were too perfect as they were—that marriage might spoil them. With that had to be content. She was greatly interested in flying —as a matter of fact, she knew quite a lot about it.

"It was shortly after this that I discovered that I'd stepped into a well-laid trap. We'd left Carmel and were living at my estate in Burlingame. One night after too much to drink I found myself talking about plans for a new engine for planes—a revolutionary idea. I won't tell you any more than that because of the secrecy necessary at this time. I did talk to her, however, because she showed such an intelligent interest and was so understanding."

"Go on," I urged with a writer's impatience because his story was running so true to form.

"In the morning Zara had gone," he said.

"And had taken the plans of the motor," I added.

"Yes. Fortunately they were not complete plans, but they were too valuable to lose, and much too important to be out of my hands.

"Later she called me from Los Angeles, said she had the plans and needed ten thousand dollars, that unless I sent the money she would be forced to sell the plans to a foreign power. Of course, I sent her the money."

"Were you planning to sell or manufacture your motor for the government of the United States?" I asked.

"Certainly, who else?"

I liked the way he said that and showed my approval.

"The government was and still is very interested in the motor."

"In that case, why didn't you get in touch with the Secret Service? I'm sure they could have got the plans back and squelched any publicity she might have wanted to give out. An invention such as yours would be a powerful weapon in the hands of an enemy country."

"I know—but the plans were not complete—she knew that. I should have notified the authorities but . . . Well, I was in love with her and didn't want to get her into trouble."

"And she, knowing that, didn't come through?"

"No. She neglected to return the plans."

"But she was to return them to you tonight for another ten thousand, is that right?"

"Yes. She promised that this would be the last ten thousand. She was to return the plans to me at the time she received the money."

"And you believed her?" It was Vicky who asked the question.

He looked at her for a moment. "Oddly enough, I did."

"Beats me how some women can get away with murder," she said and shook her head bewildered.

"If you had known that she was in desperate straits would you have given her the ten thousand without the plans?"

"I would have given her anything, and she knew it, but this time I meant to have the plans. She had to do what she did, Mallory. I honestly believe that she had to have intrigue and excitement to keep her alive. Taking my plans was a game with her. You've known people who can't tell the truth, must lie, for no reason at all?" At my nod he went on, "She was like that. All life was a game. She had to be the central point, had to control, pull strings, be important in her own eyes, like a child."

I heard Vicky mumble, "Some baby," but I ignored that.

"You were looking for the plans when we found you in her cabin earlier this evening? Did you have any luck?"

"None at all—couldn't find a trace of them, yet I'm certain she had them on board with her."

"Have you any idea about the money she seemed to need so desperately?"

He was slow to answer, quite reluctant, but I waited.

"Nothing definite, Mallory—just a suspicion that I wouldn't care to voice because I've nothing in the way of proof."

"Would it have anything to do with the row at Ciro's?" I asked.

"It might. I suspected Sarakov."

I gave him an encouraging smile. "That's all we have to go on—suspicions. From them we may work out the puzzle and find the solution. I'll donate a clue that may possibly supply the missing link. She was being blackmailed and not by Sarakov."

The dawn of understanding flashed across his face — he seemed relieved.

"While that, of course, doesn't supply an absolute proof—still it makes me feel that I should tell you why I suspected Sarakov. After I'd received the first demand from her, I went to the manager of the night club. As I've already told you, he was under an obligation to me; I cornered him and told him that, unless he told me all he knew about her, I would call the loan I'd made him. We both knew that would put him out of business. After a great deal of beating about the bush I learned that a friend of his, Michael Sarakov, had brought her with him from the Orient. Also that this man Sarakov had got his friend to feature her in his night club floor show for the express purpose of meeting me. I've since learned that the manager of the club, a man named Ivan Krassin, was a former captain in Van Ungern's White Army and, since coming to this country, has been suspected of having connections with a powerful Oriental nation. He has been under surveillance of the Secret Service for some months."

I brought forth her handkerchief, opened it, and handed him the piece of blue paper. "Does that mean anything to you?"

He studied that small slip of paper. His face lit up. "Definitely, it's my writing, it's the corner from the plans she stole from me. Where are they? Where did you get this?"

"The plans have been burned, you've nothing to worry about now but your ten thousand dollars. I think we may get that too."

A far-away look filled his eyes. He spoke slowly. He said, "She was white after all."

If Vicky grunted I chose to pay no attention to it.

I, like Vicky, doubted it but there was no need to tell him what I thought. My guess was that she'd have kept bleeding him, if she could. She had burned the plans for a very good reason of her own. That reason, if I could get to it, would be the answer to the riddle. He looked very tired.

'Try and get some sleep," I suggested.

He was glad to leave. After he had gone I sat looking at the door for a long time.

"What gives?" Rocky asked.

"Plenty."

"Why didn't you ask him for full particulars about the row at Ciro's last night?" Vicky demanded.

"I'm not curious about that. I'm wondering about other angles. We're in a mess, boys and girls. I don't like the feel of this thing now. That Purple Domino crowd is bad medicine. There have been a lot of stories circulated about it. This is more than just a murder. I wonder just how Sarakov fits into the picture. If he is a spy we will probably end with our throats slit."

Rocky whistled. "The F.B.I. ought to handle this," he said.

"And rest assured," I told him, "if there was any way to get them over here tonight, I'd do it. Zara was murdered because of those plans. She was playing all ends against the middle, trying to get away with it. I don't like it. For our own safety I don't want anyone to know that we know about the plans. I think we'd better put this little box back in her cabin. Will you do it, Rocky, and be sure you wipe your fingerprints off. Just put it on her dressing-table."

CHAPTER SEVEN

I WAS THINKING about the possibilities of the case while I waited for Rocky to bring Sid in. I had asked Rocky to scout around and find a pad and some pencils. He had galloped off like a Great Dane. I pulled a table over to the settee and sat down.

Vicky came to sit beside me, looked up at me a moment and then put her head in my lap and went to sleep. The Peke pillowed himself on her chest and followed suit—he knew a swell spot when he saw it.

I couldn't get Grey out of my mind. His story seemed genuine enough. He admitted that she had made a fool out of him. It was the old vampire story done in modern times. He had admitted that he would have done anything for her, and yet, he had definitely stated that he meant to have the plans. He had been worried about them as a good American should have been. I didn't want to, but I had to admit that it was quite possible that Grey might have killed her because of the plans. He had motive. He had had opportunity. He had been in the water at the time of the contest. He was something of an athlete too. You know the type of man who when approaching middle age tries in every way possible to recapture his receding youth. Grey was like that. He probably had a gym in his home and spent hours keeping himself fit. If he had killed her, however, would he have used curare and did he know about the diving party ahead of time? That would be one of the questions I must ask Sid.

In a little while Rocky returned with the perspiring Sid in tow. He deposited several sheets of foolscap on the table and four pencils. Perhaps he thought I was going to start another novel. When he put them on the table he plunked them down hard and awakened Vicky.

She sat up and blinked. The Peke rolled into her lap without waking—the drunken sot.

"I thought you'd gone to sleep," I said.

She yawned. "Nope! Going to help you." She picked up a pencil and about half of the paper.

"Darling," I said, "don't you think you'd better—"

"Go to sleep?" She finished it for me. "No—I'm going to help you and you're going to like it."

I looked at Rocky, and he motioned toward the room where Betty'd been. I shook my head. No—that was out. I was willing to try to solve the mystery but I'd be damned of I'd risk losing out with Vicky on account of it—not after the incident in her cabin.

I turned to Sid. "We may as well start with your investigation."

He didn't seem very enthusiastic.

"I suppose so, Dean. Well—I'm your victim."

"Let's hope it will be painless," I said.

His large eyes popped—thyroid case, I imagine. "With me? Why, Dean?"

"That's just what I want to find out. Have a seat." Rocky shoved a chair over and sat Sid down in it.

"How long've you known Zara?"

He fidgeted a bit in his chair. "Do you have to do this to me, Dean?"

"Yes. How long?"

"About a year."

"Where'd you meet her?"

"At the Purple Domino in Frisco."

"What were you doing there?"

"It's a place to go, everybody knows that. It's supposed to be hot."

"It was for you, wasn't it? But never mind about that. Did Zara ever mention any enemies to you?"

"No."

"What do you know about her past?"

"Only what she told me. That her father was a Russian nobleman, that he was killed by the Bolsheviks.

You read all about it, it was in all the papers."

"I read what your publicity man wrote—if that's what you mean. We'll skip that for the moment. Tell me—what were your relations with her?"

His lower lip started to droop. "What do you mean? There was nothing between us. You know me, Dean — always business with me, not monkey business like a lot of the other boys," he added.

"Then you don't consider marriage a relationship?"

His jaw sagged visibly. He wilted.

"You've got too much imagination," he said.

"Listen, Sid, quit stalling. Four months ago you married her in Mexicali, didn't you?"

"Well, what if I did? That's my business—ain't it?" he asked sullenly.

"Sure it's your business, Sid. I'm sorry I had to know about it. But, why did you marry her? You must have known that she didn't love you?" That was an unnecessary thrust and I was sorry I had made it.

Tears came into his eyes. "She told me she loved me, Dean. She said that looks weren't everything, that she loved me for my brains." Then he added sadly, "I thought that, maybe, if I made a big star out of her, I could make her happy."

"Then at the time you married her, you really thought she loved you?"

"Yes, Dean, I believed her, and since then I've done all I could for her. Wasn't she to play the lead in *Blue Lagoon?*"

He'd been more than square with her. I felt sorry for him.

"I know, Sid, you did all you could to make her happy—but she didn't shoot square with you."

His head sagged forward, tears trickled down his cheeks.

"I know, Dean, but what could I do? I don't blame her—she was young and beautiful. She wasn't really a bad girl."

"Just playful," Vicky suggested with some of that same irony she had displayed in front of Grey.

I liked the way he defended her. I hated to browbeat him in this way, but it had to be done.

"Any way you look at it, Sid, you were on a spot. You were married to her, and you knew she was stepping out, cheating. She was under contract to you and for some reason you wanted your marriage kept a secret. Why did you?"

"Well . . . Because my own divorce hadn't become final," he admitted in desperation.

"So you hired someone to kill her, eh? She had you by the whiskers and that was your only way out."

"No! No! No! That's a lie. I tell you I loved her! I wouldn't have hurt a hair on her head. You must believe that, Dean!" He was very excited.

I reached over and patted him on the shoulder. "Take it easy, Sid," I said. "This is just a formula that has to be gone through."

"You think you're writing a book," he accused. He made an effort at pulling himself together.

"I wish it were a book. I don't like this."

"Much!" Vicky scoffed.

I passed that one and said, "This publicity stunt—you told me it was your idea. Was the part about the Rajah throwing the junk into the water also your idea?"

"Well—not exactly. Carl Waetjen suggested that—he's a good publicity man, knows what the public wants."

I remembered Carl, an inoffensive little fellow with a large family—hardly the murderer type. I hadn't seen him on the yacht. "Where is he now?" I asked.

"He went to New York last week for the opening of *Black Lightning.*"

That of course gave Carl a clean bill.

"Who else, besides you and Waetjen, knew that this was only a publicity stunt?"

He thought a moment. "Well—Frank Lane knew about it, and, of course, the Rajah, and I told you."

"Did anyone else know in advance that the Rajah was going to throw alleged rubies overboard?"

"Sarakov. It was from him I got the idea. He told me about diving for pearls in the South Seas."

"Is he a friend of yours, Sid?"

"I don't know. How can I tell who my friends are when so many people are looking for favors? He was her friend. He was nice to me. She wanted him on the party. So did I, because he's the only one who could handle her when she had a tantrum."

"And you expected a tantrum?"

"She was like nitro-glycerine. You never knew when she'd blow up."

"Was it generally known that there would be swimming?"

"I told everybody to bring bathing suits, said we might want to shoot some pictures for the papers."

"What about Grey? Did he know about this stunt?"

"How could he know? I didn't tell him."

"Do you know why Grey and Sarakov quarreled last night?"

"It was because of her but I don't know why. She never told me anything."

"Okay, Sid. Stick around. I may want you later—don't swim away," I kidded.

"Fat chance—I'm no Johnny Weissmuller." With that summary of his physical prowess he left us.

If he hadn't made that last crack I wouldn't have remembered. I'd forgotten about Sid at the time of the murder. He was in the water and while he was no Weissmuller true enough, yet he was in the water at the time she died. I had seen him coming up the ladder a weird sight in his bathing suit. He was frightened too.

"What goes on in the noble dome?" Vicky asked.

"I was just thinking about Sarakov and his pearl diving."

"Want me to bring him in?" Rocky asked eagerly.

"No, let's have talk with the Rajah."

CHAPTER EIGHT

WHILE I'D BEEN cross-questioning Sid, Vicky had been busy with her pencil and paper. I glanced over to see what she'd done. She'd done quite a bit, she had drawn a darn good profile of Rocky, had given him everything he had and an added quality of fineness.

'That's swell, Vicky. I knew you were going to be a great help to me," I said.

She said, "Hush! I'm thinking."

I hoped all her thoughts were not centered on Rocky. I flipped the end of her ear with my finger and said I was sorry for interrupting the séance. She gave me a tap on the arm which meant that I was forgiven.

Rocky came in with the Rajah. He was still minus his collar and tie. I told him to sit down.

"To save a lot of time," I began, "I'll tell you that we know this was only a publicity stunt, and that you're not the Rajah of Benang. Who are you?"

The man dropped his haughty demeanor, relaxed, grinned easily and said, "My name's Julma Desa."

"Is that the name you use at Central Casting?"

"It is also my real name."

"Where were you born?"

"In Ciudad, Bolivar on the Orinoco."

I raised my eyebrows at this.

"Rather a long way from India, isn't it?"

"Yes. My parents settled there a long time ago. They are from India but went there for political reasons. My father made a living by mixing herbs, at which he was very skilful. He doctored the natives and the poor people."

"Then you know about curare?"

His eyes darkened. "Yes."

"Did you know that Zara was poisoned by curare?"

He seemed surprised or else was a darned good actor.

He shook his head. "No—I did not know that. I have seen people die from it—they die quickly."

I agreed with that statement. "You didn't by any chance bring any of the poison with you?"

He smiled gravely. "No. I am a Hindu. I do not believe in violence—I did not kill the girl Zara."

"How long have you known her?"

"I have heard about her, of course, but I met her for the first time this afternoon when she came on the yacht as my guest."

"How many people did you tell about this job of yours?"

"Only my wife. I was cautioned to say nothing about it by Mr. Tricker."

"You told no one that there was going to be a diving contest?"

"No. I did not know about it until after I'd given the necklace to Zara. Then Mr. Tricker told me about it and gave me the bag of rubies."

This was news. According to Sid, both he and his publicity man Waetjen had decided on the diving contest several days previously. Why then was the Rajah not told about it until practically the last minute?

It might be perfectly all right—on the other hand it might have a very definite bearing on the case. I made a note to question Sid about it. I told the man that he could go, that I'd call him again if I needed him.

Rocky came over after he had gone. His big face was screwed into thoughtful knots.

"Y'know, Chief—there's something fishy about that bird. Them Ethiopians—you can't trust 'em." I didn't check him on that. 'They're tricky. I wouldn't be surprised if he's the one that killed her. He may have hypnotized the crowd into thinking he was on deck, when all the time he was overboard murdering the girl."

"Sorry, Rocky—you're wrong there. Miss Blaire tore his collar and tie off during the excitement. QUICK! *At the window—get him!*"

I'd just caught a glimpse of a face at one of the windows. It was open—it was a hot night inside. I couldn't tell whether it was a man or a woman. It was just a flash as if someone were flattened against the edge of the window listening. The moment I called the face vanished.

Rocky spun on his heel and charged. He flung open the first door and plunged through. A bellow announced he'd got some place. He had. He'd landed in the washroom in his excitement. Meanwhile I'd started across for the door, forgetting that I was still tied to Vicky. I brought up sharply, yanking her half across the table. Shang went flying from her lap and slid along the floor bringing down an ash receiver in transit. I apologized to Vicky—she was laughing so hard that the tears were streaming down her cheeks.

Shang picked himself up, gave me a dirty look and waddled back to Vicky. She lifted the little fellow up and put him back in her lap. It was a hell of a way to treat a guy with a hang-over. Rocky stumbled back into the lounge looking very sheepish.

"Where's that blankety-blank door?" he shouted. "I'll get the so-and-so . . ." He surged ahead to the deck.

"Hold it, Rocky," I called. "It's no use now, whoever was there is gone by this time. We made enough racket to scare a herd of elephants."

Vicky looked across at me. "It's like a book, Dean. For a while I thought nothing was going to happen. It's been slow and not very interesting."

"That," I reminded her, "is because in real life things don't happen with calculated speed. Besides, I don't know the answer to this little riddle."

"And you won't from the way we're going," she said doubtfully.

"It takes time, lady," Rocky suggested helpfully.

"And patience," I added. "We've got to find a logical motive before we can begin to get anywhere. This murder was not a crime of passion. It was well planned in advance and I want to know why."

"That face at the window," she said. "Doesn't sound so good to me, Dean. Look! I'll marry you, take a chance. Forget the riddle. You don't have to prove anything to me. I know you're good. Let Rocky solve the crime, it's his job. If I'm going to take you for better or worse, and it will probably be the worst, I'd like to have you all in one piece. I like you the way you are."

Those were very heartening words but I wasn't very romantic about it. My mind was too full of other things. Instead of showing my pleasure at her capitulation I said, "I don't want to quit now. It's beginning to get interesting. I'm in no danger yet. I haven't hit a sure thing but the curare and the fact that Julma Desa is a Hindu who was born in South America."

"Maybe he was the guy at the window," Rocky suggested.

"It's possible that he stopped for a look," I admitted. "Now while I'm getting us out of this tangle suppose you find Basil St. Denis for me."

"Why St. Denis?" Vicky demanded as I tried to undo the knot which bound us together.

"I'm superstitious about this rope," she said. "Sort of like it."

"So do I," I agreed, "but if we're not careful we'll break our necks with it or worse." I cussed a little as I worked over the knot. It wouldn't budge, so I ambled to the table for the knife which had killed Zara.

It was gone. I had more cursing to do then for my stupidity, but I did it inwardly. What a fool I had been to leave it there for the murderer to find and dispose of in any way he chose.

At last the knot came apart. "At least I didn't cut it," I said as I coiled the rope and tossed it to the couch beside her. "While you're getting yourself out of it tell me what you think of Henry Grey's story," I suggested.

She gave me a funny look and said, "Well, Sherlock — far be it from me to have an evil mind, but—you can't make me believe that a hard-boiled business man like Henry Grey would hand out wads of money like that just because he was in love with the girl—platonic friendships don't start in dear Hollywood before the ripe old age of eighty."

"He didn't say it was platonic."

"But he gave it that touch of sweetness," she insisted.

"Could be," I said. "I read of a case in the paper a few days ago. A man of eighty-seven was arrested for rape but he claimed just a friendly interest."

She smiled mischievously up at me and said, "It must have been a mental case."

"You win," I said and bowed politely. She noticed the crown of my head. My hair is getting a trifle thin up there. I'd been using bear-grease on it, at least that's what the label said it was—personally I think it's a by-product of some riding academy. Anyway Vicky noticed the hair.

"Getting a trifle thin on the solarium, professor—that is a direct result of too much indulgence in the sinful lusts of the flesh."

"It's been like that since I was eighteen—premature baldness—runs in the family. Will you love me when I'm bald, honey child?"

She leaned over, kissed me and whispered, "Maybe— if I massage it every night."

She saw the grin on my face. We'll skip the next half-minute of our conversation.

Our foolishness was interrupted by the arrival of my faithful bloodhound with St. Denis. He nodded to us, parked his elegant body and lit a cigarette. He was a nice enough fellow, but as I've said before, a bit conceited.

"You wanted to see me, Mallory?"

"Just a few questions. When they lined up for the diving—where were you?"

"I was at the end of the line—the opposite one from Zara."

"I saw you come up once. You seemed rather frantic.

Had you noticed anything unusual?"

"Can't say I did. I was out of breath. I saw a ruby settling on the bottom and went after it. Here it is." He put his hand in a trouser pocket and brought out a piece of red glass. "After that I came up for air, then went under again to try to find another, but didn't have any luck."

"Well, don't make a present of it to your best girl—it's only glass, one of Sid's little jokes." A sickly look stole over his face. He'd evidently thought the Rajah and the jewels to be the real thing.

"That's just like that little so-and-so—and his lousy stunt cost Zara her life!" he cried bitterly.

"You thought a lot of her, didn't you?"

"She loved me," he said.

"Tell me—how long had you known her?"

"About ten months—ever since she came on the Tricker lot."

"And you knew her quite well—didn't you?" I could see him stiffen. "Took her out a lot too, didn't you?"

"Yes, she was to be my leading lady—there was nothing wrong about taking her out."

"So you thought you were top in her eyes?" I asked.

"I know I was," he boasted.

"Are you quite sure about that? Had you no idea about the other men in her life, Grey, Sarakov, the rug peddler? How could you have been so blind?"

"I wasn't blind. I . . ."

I stared at him for a few seconds. He was getting nervous, realized that his admission might be construed as a motive, one of the greatest—jealousy. He kept flicking the ash from the end of his cigarette. Finally I put another question.

"It seems to me that I heard, not so long ago, that you were engaged to Naomi Ravelle—was that so?"

He hesitated—then answered cautiously, "We had a sort of an understanding—but it wasn't official."

"I see—you gave up the idea shortly after you met

Zara."

He flushed angrily. "What are you driving at?" he demanded.

"That Zara made a fool out of you, played with you for some purpose of her own, that you found it out, realized what she had done to you, knew that you were in a bad way because of her and might lose everything —Naomi, your chance for a career, your reputation. You wanted her out of the way," I accused.

"No! Good God, no!"

"There's no need to get so excited," I assured him. "When there's been a murder committed every angle must be explored and lots of unpleasant questions have to be asked—it can't be helped."

"And I don't see why you should be the one to ask them. After all you're nothing but a writer." There was no effort to keep contempt out of his voice. "And you've been seen around with Zara, spent a lot of time in her bungalow on the lot; so much so, that"—he paused for dramatic effect—"there was talk, and stories on the lot, bare facts I might add."

I didn't look at Vicky, didn't want to. There'd be a game of questions and answers a little later, and knowing Vicky the answers would have to be very good.

"All of which has nothing to do with this evening's happenings," I reminded him. "I was not in the water when Zara was killed."

I thought he turned a shade paler. After his little digression about Zara and myself I enjoyed seeing him squirm.

"Does that make me a suspect?" he asked with an assumption of ease.

"You and a few others."

"And just so you don't get any wrong ideas," Rocky cut in, "Mr. Mallory is my special deputy to ask questions. Get it?"

"But even your power doesn't give him the right to accuse me or anyone else of murder." He gave Rocky a less-than-the-dust look and turned back to me.

"Wasn't Zamper next to you?" I asked.

"You mean the funny-looking runt with the curved legs?"

I nodded. "What do you know about him?"

He seemed glad to have the center of interest veer away from him—odd for an actor but true nevertheless.

"She said he was an old friend of hers. He hung around her quite a bit. I never knew why. I asked her once but she brushed the question off. So I thought it was probably something she didn't want to talk about. I never asked her again. He used to peddle Oriental rugs and jewelry among the picture crowd. I bought a rug from him—a beautiful thing—but I found later that I could've bought one like it at Barker Brothers for half the price."

I thanked him for the information and told him he could go back to his cabin, the bar or . . .

As soon as he'd left, Rocky uncorked. "That's the bird who didn't commit the murder—the guy's a, you know," he gave a shy look at Vicky, "one of the boys."

I agreed with him—about being the murderer I mean—and asked him to get Naomi Ravelle.

I wasn't looking forward to cross-questioning Naomi. She was well liked by the picture crowd and had the peerless reputation of being very good-hearted and generous. True to her Latin blood, she had a temper. I'd seen it in action on a few occasions and was thankful not to be on the receiving end. But for a girl who basked in the celluloid spotlight she was pretty regular.

I had uncovered something in her past; so had Zara. They had had a row. Naomi had been furious out there on the deck earlier in the evening, might have killed Zara then if it had not been for Sarakov. She was a fine girl with a wild temper and so constituted that she would fight for the thing she wanted. I believed she wanted two things, Basil St. Denis and the safety of her child.

I was not liking my detective role at the moment but I had to go on with it. I could not have stopped then had I wanted to do so.

CHAPTER NINE

ROCKY WAS BEAMING when he ushered Naomi into the lounge. She looked stunning. She wore a turquoise blue negligee which was a perfect frame for her exotic, cafe-au-lait coloring. She'd evidently made a hit with Rocky. The big egg held the chair for her and was rewarded with a dazzling smile which sent him down for the count.

She turned to me and said lightly, "Well, Dean—turning real detective?"

I smiled. "Hardly, Naomi—just a few questions. I'm helping Mr. Stonehead and he has graciously suggested that I take the initiative. First, tell me—how long have you know Zara?"

"Ever since she came on the Tricker lot—about ten months."

"Sid gave her the lead in *Blue Lagoon* in your place, didn't he?"

I noticed a slight tightening of her lips.

"Everyone knows that," she said.

"You didn't like her, did you?"

Faint traces of a sneer touched the corners of her lovely mouth.

"Frankly—no!"

"Why?"

"For many reasons. Her sudden success went to her head, she acted as if she owned the studio—and everyone in it. She was ruthless, went after the things she wanted."

"Do you refer to Basil?"

My shot went home. She flushed—then quickly regained her poise. But I could hear a small foot tapping nervously on the floor.

"Partly that. He was fascinated by her. But I think it

was chiefly on account of Sid and the part. You know the picture business, Dean, how it works. I didn't mind so much about Basil. When two people are going to be starred together they usually try to fake a romance for the public. I didn't think it was just a stunt. She had what men like."

It was a comment rather than a statement of fact but I saw Vicky shoot me a quick glance. She was doing some mental bookkeeping, that child, and I was going to be definitely in the red.

"All men?" I asked.

"You ought to know," Naomi replied.

She wasn't mean about it, didn't overemphasize the point as St. Denis had done, didn't pause, just went on talking.

"Basil is an artist. With him his work comes first. After all, he is an actor and publicity is the thing that keeps him and the rest of us going."

She was sticking up for Denis nobly.

"Yes, I know about that—it's the usual thing. Would you say this—er—publicity stunt was the reason for breaking off the engagement between you and Basil?"

Her eyes flashed angrily.

"That's entirely my own affair."

She glared defiantly at me. While I'd been questioning her I'd pulled the photograph of her with the baby from my robe. I now slid it across the table.

"And this, I suppose, is also your affair?"

I'd caught her off guard. As soon as she saw the picture she gave a little choking cry. "Where did you get this?"

"I found it in a drawer in Zara's wardrobe trunk."

She made no reply—just stared at the photograph.

I continued, "Any idea how she got hold of it? I'm sure you didn't give it to her."

She raised her eyes. They were filled with tears. "No, Dean, I've no idea and I don't want to think that . . ." Her lower lip trembled a little. I felt that she was thinking of

Basil.

"Listen, Naomi—I'm going to be very frank with you. You're in a bad spot. First of all, you were next to her when the diving started. Second, you admit that you disliked her. After all, she had been given the lead in *Blue Lagoon* which had originally been slated for you. And, she had taken the man you loved—the father of your child."

The poor girl went deathly pale, I thought she was going to faint. With superhuman effort she controlled herself. Her voice came in a low pregnant whisper. "I would have killed her, intended to do it, Dean. Wanted to, only I waited too long. Someone else did it and, I'm glad I didn't do it, honestly I am, Dean."

"If all you say is true—what then?" I hated to put her on the spot, but it couldn't be helped. "I'm sorry I have to drag out your secrets, Naomi. I like you and I want to help you. But murder's been committed, it's nasty business and we've got to get to the bottom of it regardless of who gets hurt. You see, for every murder there has to be a motive. That's what we're trying to find in this case. So far you had every reason to wish her out of the way. It puts you in a very bad light—I wish you'd be honest with me, I might be able to help then. Now, it's just us, and we're friends. If we can finish before the police come, many things need not be known."

"That's right," Rocky added his assurance to mine.

She looked me straight in the eyes for a moment as if she were weighing me.

"All right, Dean, I will. You were quite right in thinking that Basil was the father of my baby. We were going to get married, but Zara came along and Basil was tremendously fascinated. It was while I was away having the baby. He was lonesome. She knew how to make fools of men."

"I'll say," Vicky agreed. There was an exchange of understanding glances between them.

"Basil must have told her about us, the baby,

everything, probably showed her the picture. When I returned I found that he practically lived at her apartment. I don't think she really loved him—I think she just wanted to hurt me. This afternoon as I was walking along the deck she called to me. She was in her cabin window. She held up this photograph for me to see and said, 'Cute little bastard, isn't he?' I could have killed her then but I couldn't get to her. She taunted me with her laughter. If I'd made a scene she would have told everyone about my baby. Potter would have loved that."

"You're very frank about admitting that you wanted to kill her."

She tensed a moment, then said slowly: "Yes—I— could have killed her—wanted to—but I've told you that."

It was a pathetic sight seeing this proud little girl so humiliated. She had every reason for wanting Zara out of the way, but I was loath to think her guilty. The murder seemed too well and calculatingly planned for one of her temperament. I could picture her tearing into Zara like a tigress, on the spur of the moment, defending her child's name and reputation—but I couldn't somehow picture her resorting to Borgian tactics. I decided to change the subject a trifle.

"Early this evening just before the diving stunt started you asked me for a cigarette. You appeared to be very nervous. Any reason?"

"I'd rather not answer that."

"You mean you're shielding someone?"

"Perhaps."

"Besides yourself, did Zara have any other enemies?"

"I don't know. I should think so."

"Then you don't think that the toast she gave might have been prompted by some premonition of death?"

"No. I remarked at the time that she was just trying to pull something unusual."

"Just a short time before that you met her on the deck. Words passed between you. She slapped your face, remember?"

Her eyes widened. "That's right—but how did you know about it? Did Michael tell you?"

"No, he didn't. Now, one other thing. Do you know anything about her past—before she came to Hollywood?"

"Nothing but the fact that she was a singer in a night club where Sid picked her up."

"Did you know she had the photograph before you came on board?"

"No."

"And you know nothing else about her?"

"Only what the publicity man gave out—a lot of hokum about her father being a Russian nobleman."

"How do you know it's hokum?"

She smiled. "I know Waetjen."

I shoved a piece of paper over to her and gave her a pencil. "Mind giving me a sample of your handwriting?"

I wanted to compare it with the note Shang had found under the bed in Zara's cabin.

She picked up the pencil. "What do you want me to write?"

I told her anything but her autograph. For a moment the pencil scratched across the paper. Then she put it down.

I said, "Thank you. You may go now, Naomi—and don't worry. I'll do my best to see that your secret doesn't get out."

Her eyes thanked me. Rocky did the honors with her chair as she rose. Halfway across the lounge I called out, "Oh! By the way!" She stopped and turned to face me. "Do you know anything about curare?"

A puzzled little frown creased her forehead. Presently she answered, "It's a poison, isn't it?"

I nodded, sorry that she should know.

"Yes, ever see any of it?"

"Once—about a week ago." I pricked up my ears.

"Where was that?"

"At Michael Sarakov's house. He has a laboratory there where he experiments with animals—vivisection.

It's a hobby of his."

"Do you remember the color of it?"

"Yellow. It was a powder."

"That must have been curarine, the commercial form of curare," I suggested.

She shrugged.

"You're sure you didn't see any that was black?" I was watching her face closely.

"No. I don't think so. Oh, yes—there was some black stuff there. I remember because I picked up a tiny rabbit that was lying unconscious on the operating table. When I put it down I noticed some sticky black stuff on my finger. Michael noticed it also. He seemed quite upset and made me clean my hands with alcohol."

"Did he give you any explanation?"

"He examined my fingers carefully and said he was very glad that I didn't have any cuts. But why do you ask?"

"Curare was used to kill Zara."

She gave a low cry—her hands flew to her mouth. Naomi was inherently loyal—she realized she had inadvertently brought her friend Sarakov under suspicion. She turned and ran sobbing from the room.

"Ain't life hell?" soliloquized Rocky as he started after the retreating girl. "A swell dame like that in a tough spot, and that blankety-blank pansy won't marry her. And here's me that'd give ten years off my life if she'd have me." He turned to me. "Say, Chief— you don't think she done it—do you? It'd be a crime to hang a beautiful girl like that."

I agreed that it would be horrible, but for him to remember his friend Cleopatra. He subsided. I asked Vicky what she thought of Naomi.

"I like her. Even if she did kill Zara, which I doubt. I'm all for her and I think her baby's cute. Did you take a good look at it?"

"You're a big help," I said.

Meanwhile I was comparing Naomi's handwriting

with the note Shang had found in Zara's cabin. I drew a blank there. Naomi's writing was a firm backhand, while that of the note was a sloping indefinite scrawl. Of course, either writing might have been disguised. I'm no handwriting expert but I felt that Naomi's was her own. She had written six words—"Help me to protect my baby."

CHAPTER TEN

ROCKY WENT TO GET Sarakov. Vicky seemingly had some unfinished business. We went to her cabin.

While I waited I thought about that missing knife. It had been carelessness on my part to allow it to be taken. I also thought about the difference between real crimes and those of imagination. The pattern was not the same, the pieces did not fit into the well-ordered scheme of an author's mind.

Frank Lane passed silently, moved on into the mist.

Presently Vicky came out fortified under a new layer of powder and lipstick. "It's spooky, this fog," she said as she took my arm. "I don't like it, Dean."

Neither did I but I didn't comment on the fact. We had just started back for the lounge when I saw someone moving in the shadow of a ventilator ahead of us. I say saw—that is hardly true. The mist seemed thicker in one spot than it had been a second before, seemed to take shape and surge like some great glob of protoplasm.

I felt a chill slither down my spine. It was not a natural reaction to the cold dampness of the night. It was fear, a sudden instinctive fear. Someone was watching us. I moved my arm out to sweep Vicky behind me, to shield her from anything that might come toward us.

It was at that moment that it happened. It flashed past. I caught its gleam from the light which was burning over the companionway. In thinking of Vicky I had saved my own life; there can be no question of that. I felt a tug at my sleeve and thought it was Vicky.

The strange shape in the mist moved, became less intense, vanished. I moved forward to find that my arm, or rather the sleeve of my robe, was pinned to the cabin door behind me. I shuddered. Had it been my arm instead of the sleeve I would never have moved again.

With my free hand I pulled the knife. Vicky's face came around my elbow. She gasped, horrified.

"Listen, Lieutenant," she said. "I think you're a swell fellow, and I think it's lots of fun sleuthing around with you, but if you're going to start acting screwy in the future and expose yourself to things like that, Shang and I won't play." She stepped back and asked. "Is it *the* knife?"

"Yes, the perfect specimen of the Mexican hummingbird. A friend just threw it at me."

"Well, that settles it. They can get someone else to do their high-powered snooping. I'm taking you to my cabin and I'm going to lock the door. If I have to marry a goofy author I want him to be a live one."

"That's a swell idea. But I've got to go through with this investigation now—I must be getting hot. We'll stay in the lounge with Rocky—it'll be safe there."

"All right, foolish—if you want to be a target for your toad-stabbing friends, Shang and I'll trail along and help clean up the mess. But if we're going, let's make it snappy. Your pal may borrow a gun and be back any minute."

It sounded like darn good advice. We hightailed it for the lounge, where we arrived safely, if a trifle out of breath.

I had expected to find Rocky waiting for us with the big Russian—but the lounge was empty.

We sat down at the table to wait for him to show up. To fill in time I examined the knife.

Just as I had expected, there was a black sticky substance smeared over the point. Evidently the murderer still had a supply of curare on hand, and was anxious to discourage any further sleuthing. It was the same knife which had killed Zara.

What had I discovered of importance? Why was it thrown at me? Maybe he didn't like the Mandarin robe. Just to be on the safe side I got up and closed a couple of windows. I didn't want the murderer taking a pot-shot at me while I was using the massive intellect for cross-examination. Anyway, he wasn't such a hot shot with a knife and he might hit Vicky. I hid the knife under a seat cushion for safe-keeping. There was curare on my sleeve. I cut a square out of the sleeve of the robe. I didn't want the poison loose on me anywhere.

Heavy footsteps sounded and in clumped Rocky with Sarakov. Rocky was apologetic. "Sorry I took so long, Chief. I had one hell of a time finding him."

Sarakov explained, "I'm sorry to have caused you so much trouble. I was in the stern smoking a cigarette."

I assured him that it was quite all right and to have a seat. So—both he and Frank Lane had been roaming around the decks while the knife-throwing had been going on. Well, it wouldn't do any good to accuse him of it, I had no proof and it would only put him more on his guard. The fellow seemed to have recovered his composure since I'd last seen him, when he'd carried Zara's body into the lounge and later had heard the opinion of the doctor. His eyes still held that strange, haunting look—as though constantly straining to see something in the darkness beyond the windows of the lounge.

"Mr. Sarakov," I began, "you probably know by this time that I've been given the unpleasant task of investigating the murder of Zara." He nodded gravely. "Naturally we are practically all under suspicion. There are a few questions that I want to ask you."

"I shall be happy to answer them, Mr. Mallory."

"Good! First of all I'd like to know how long you've known the dead girl."

"I met her about a year ago in San Francisco."

"And you fell in love with her?"

He hesitated, then said slowly, "Yes—in my own way I loved her."

"Did she return your love?"

His face remained expressionless. "Who can tell of a

woman's love? I expected no return."

We weren't getting very far. I tried another tack.

"Can you tell us anything about her past—before she came to California?"

"She never spoke of her past," was the quiet reply.

"I see. Well, did she have any enemies, any that you knew?"

He was silent for a moment—as though carefully weighing his answer. "I couldn't make a definite statement to such a question."

"You say you can't make a definite statement. Am I to gather from that there is some legitimate doubt in your mind?"

"Mr. Mallory—I don't like to cast suspicion on someone without sufficient proof. But I feel it my duty to tell you that there was one man that Zara seemed to dread. She never said anything about it. But her actions indicated a certain fear of the man. I have known her to go to great lengths to avoid seeing him."

Things were beginning to get interesting.

"Would you mind telling me that man's name?"

"Jan Zamper," he said slowly.

"Oh, the rug peddler!"

"Exactly! The rug peddler," he said with contempt.

"Do you mean she was afraid for her life?"

"I would not go as far as that. I think he had some hold over her—possibly something connected with her past."

"And this man Zamper—do you like him?"

He shrugged his shoulders. "I do not like him, neither do I dislike him—he comes of a class of people that one simply does not consider."

"He is a fellow-countryman of yours, isn't he?"

"No. He speaks our tongue, but very badly. He is an Armenian."

"Zara—was she a Russian?"

"I'm not sure. She spoke our tongue fluently. I think she was born in Russia, of Bohemian parents."

"Another thing—I understand you're interested in vivisection."

His face became alive for the first time.

"Yes, it is a hobby of mine."

"And a very interesting one I'm sure. Along what particular lines are you conducting your research?"

"Along a very unusual one, Mr. Mallory. When I say that vivisection is a hobby of mine I mean rather that it is a means to furthering a hobby, which is hunting with the bow and arrow. I like to be as humane as possible. It often happens that an animal is wounded and escapes— only to die a lingering death later. In the course of my experiments I have discovered a certain poison that, injected into any part of the body, creates a paralysis of the muscles almost immediately. Of course, the nearer the heart it is injected the quicker the results. Further, the meat of the animal so killed may be eaten in perfect safety. This particular poison is only deadly if injected into the blood-stream." He gave me a slow smile.

"That's very interesting—and the name of the poison?"

"Curare," he replied casually.

"Does it have definite symptoms?" I asked, equally casual.

"Quite."

"Do you use it in the commercial form or in its natural state?"

"I use both in my experiments—but for hunting I use the pure curare."

I reached under the cushion and laid the knife on the table.

"What substance would you say was on the tip and side of this blade?"

He took the knife and examined the point closely.

"It looks very much like curare," he said. Then he tasted it with the tip of his tongue. "Yes—I think it is— but I could not make a positive statement. Might I ask where the knife came from?"

"I wish I knew. It was tossed at me a few minutes ago, just before you came in, by someone who would rather I did not work on this case."

"It's my knife," he stated baldly.

"Are you sure?"

He looked again. "Reasonably sure. They are very common. I bought one to use with my fishing kit. I intend to do some fishing tomorrow with curare-baited hooks."

"Then since you have curare, admit the knife is yours, are you confessing?"

"Confessing?" he rumbled. "Why should I confess?"

I shrugged. "The knife is probably yours. It was thrown at me. You know all about curare. Rather a natural question, don't you think?"

"Natural yes, but futile. I did not throw the knife."

His was the second disarming confession I had had. First Grey and now Sarakov told me a story that would make any man suspicious. His very candor suggested a motive behind the seeming honesty of his words.

"Why didn't you tell me somebody threw a knife at you?" Rocky asked.

I smiled and told him to forget it, but to keep his eyes peeled when going along the decks. I turned back to the big Russian.

"Curare was used to kill Zara," I said. "And on that knife."

"Curare—Zara!" he mumbled.

I was watching his face closely. This time I got a definite rise out of him. His eyes dilated momentarily—then his fists clenched, and he began muttering under his breath in Russian. In a few seconds the spasm had passed and he'd regained his composure.

"Well," I prompted, "have you any comment to make?"

He made no reply—merely shrugged his shoulders again. His calm indifference made me feel that he knew a great deal more than he pretended—but intended keeping it to himself. I could not believe that a man who had been so deeply moved by her death could honestly be as callous as he seemed.

Suddenly he reached across the table and picked up a pencil and a sheet of paper. He wrote rapidly—then pushed the sheet across to me. I glanced quickly at the hurried scrawl. *"Don't turn your head. I believe someone is at the window behind you."* Was this a trick or what was it? I'd soon find out. I pushed the paper over to Rocky.

He grinned, rose slowly, walked down the length of the lounge and stepped out on deck.

Just to be on the safe side I started to question Sarakov again—I wanted to hold the eavesdropper's attention until Rocky could get into position.

"Do you have a license to practice vivisection?" I asked.

"No. I hold no degree of medicine so I doubt if I could obtain one."

"Where do you get your supply of curare?"

"The curarine I have been getting from a friend in a large research laboratory. As I do not wish to get him into trouble I will not mention his name. The curare I obtained through this man Zamper."

It was beginning to look as if Zamper would have a lot of explaining to do.

"How did you happen to get it from him?"

"It was quite accidental. Zamper does quite a business importing rare things for the motion picture people. The man claims that, given time, he can get anything. So one day I asked him if he could get me some curare. I did not hear anything from him for a couple of months and thought that he had forgotten about it. Then one day he turned up with a package containing curare. Since then . . ."

A thump and a loud scream interrupted him. From the commotion I gathered that my faithful bloodhound had gone into action. Came a lot of powerful action and hot language delivered in Rocky's now eloquent voice.

Vicky said, "Bet he's got Zamper."

"Or your pal Lane," I suggested.

We were both wrong. Rocky's huge form loomed in the door. He was propelling someone along by the scruff of the neck—it was our old friend Betty Potter. The lady was more than perturbed. She was so damned mad she was inarticulate. I turned to Sarakov and told him he could leave, that if I needed him again I'd send for him, and warned him to stay close to his cabin.

He stood up, towering over me, and I'm not exactly a small person.

"I am perhaps under technical arrest then?" he asked—an amused smile on his face.

"I'm merely conducting an investigation for Mr. Stonehead, Mr. Sarakov. I suggested that you remain in your cabin so that we could get hold of you quickly in case we needed you for further questioning."

"And what he says goes," Rocky added.

"I understand perfectly, Mr. Mallory."

He bowed stiffly and strode out of the lounge, ignoring Rocky rather magnificently.

Betty Potter found her voice immediately.

"For God's sake, tell your gorilla to let go my dress before he pulls all my clothes off," she shrilled.

The huge hand holding her dress dropped, as if struck by lightning. He looked at his paw while she shook her rumpled clothing into a semblance of respectability. Judging by the contours Rocky must have broken something of vital importance to her upper deck. The old girl did sail close-hauled.

I asked, "Snooping again, eh, Betty?"

"That's my business," she snapped.

"You're telling me? Well, I hope you got a good earful."

"Maybe I did—but it'll be nothing compared with what I'll spill after I get off this damned boat." She glanced meaningly at Vicky.

Vicky returned her smile. It was sickeningly sweet about the lips but there were poisoned darts in her eyes.

"I'll make a bargain with you, Betty. Oh, no—not the

kind you think I mean." I could see her getting that cat-that-ate-the-canary look on her face. "The bargain I have in mind is this: If you will answer a few questions and then go and stay in your cabin and stop getting in our hair, I will promise to give you the whole story about Zara's murder as soon as I get it. It'll be your beat—and a damn big one."

I'd touched her weak spot. No matter what else she was, she was all newspaper when it came to news or story. She began to unbend. Then she was in the chair opposite—her professional smile once more in place.

"Okay, Mr. Mastermind—shoot."

I let that crack pass.

"How long had you been outside the window before we spotted you?"

"I'd only just got there."

She looked peaked—so I guessed she was telling the truth.

"Was that the first time you'd been there?"

"Yes. Has anyone else been listening?"

"I thought you might have tried it before. I know how newspaper people are," I said.

"It wasn't me the other time," she stated.

"Who put you up to listening this time?" I asked. That got a rise out of her.

"Say, who d'you think you're talking to? I've got brains of my own."

"Listen, Betty—you're not keeping your part of the bargain. Someone tipped you off and I want to know who it was."

She looked at me almost with respect, certainly with wonder.

"Well—if you must know—it was Frank Lane."

"I see. Frank Lane asked you to listen in and then report everything that's floated into your shell-like ear, is that it?"

"He said he'd like to know what was going on."

"All right, Betty—that explains that. Now—do you

know anything that might shed some light on this mess?"

"No. It's as much a mystery to me as it is to you, maybe more so."

"Dear Betty," I thought, "That was a coy dig, bless your heart, you worm."

"I can't imagine why anyone wanted to kill that poor girl—unless it was the aftermath of some love affair," she suggested so aptly that I smelled a leading question.

"Did she have many?" I asked.

Betty raised an eyebrow. "Did she have many? My deah Mr. Mallory, where have you been?"

The old girl was getting back into her stride. All she had to do was to see you talking to a girl and she'd have you both tagged for a romance and at least one illegitimate offspring. I had visions of what was in store for Vicky and myself unless I did something to quiet her.

"Interesting—if true, but that doesn't help very much. Tell me—what do you know of her past? Before she came to Hollywood, I mean."

"Why—" She changed her mind and went on, "Just that Sid found her in a night club in San Francisco—beyond that nothing."

"You're quite sure of that, Betty?" I insisted because I suspected her of holding back.

"Yes—oh, I almost forgot. A man came to me a few months ago with a proposition. He claimed that he had some very interesting information about her past, and wanted to know if I'd write it up for newspaper syndicate publication on a fifty-fifty basis. I told him that if it was hot enough I would. The next time I saw him he made no mention of it, and when I asked him about it he laughed and said he'd only been kidding."

"And when you saw him and he told you that, he had blossomed out, he had a car and a chauffeur, was doing nicely for himself. The man was Jan Zamper and he didn't need your money, is that right?"

"Yes," she admitted. "How did you know? Did he tell you?"

At last, her admission gave me an important piece in the jigsaw puzzle—something tangible to work on.

"What do you know about this fellow Zamper?"

"Well—he imports Oriental rugs and things which he peddles around the studios. I felt sorry for him and got him a few customers."

"On a commission basis?" I asked.

"No, sweetheart—I took it out in trade," she snapped sarcastically.

"Is he doing pretty well in this business?"

"When he first arrived—about a year or so ago—he was having a tough time, that was . . ."

"Yes, yes," I cut in impatiently, "that was why you helped him out. Go on!"

She favored me with a dirty look.

"As I was saying, he had a tough time in the beginning. However, about six months ago he did get a high-powered limousine and chauffeur."

"Yes," I said to myself, "about the time Henry Grey loaned Zara the ten thousand dollars. Wouldn't you like to get your teeth in that story!" I said to her, "Do you know where Zamper lives?"

"I don't know the exact address, but I've been there a few times—on business of course. He rooms in a small house on one of the side roads off the upper end of Benedict Canyon. The fellow who's playing the part of the Rajah owns it."

"You mean Julma Desa? Then you knew he was a phony, that the whole party was a . . ."

"My dear Mallory, don't be childish. After all, I've been around this town for years and years." She smiled with condescension a moment, then changed her manner. "If you know so much—why the hell are you taking up my time?"

"Because, lovely, I like to listen to your silvery voice."

"Oh yeah?" She was beginning to get nasty again.

"Now, Betty—be a good little girl and run along to your cabin and stay there. If I find you've talked to Frank

Lane there'll be no scoop for you."

"Not much chance of there being any with a dumb cluck like you working on the case. Did I know the party was a fake? My God! I invented these damn phony parties!"

"Before you go, Mrs. Edison, would you mind telling me why she took a sock at you? Zara, I mean."

She glared, was a little startled I think.

"It wasn't just a love tap," I suggested with a reminiscent smile. "What did you have on her, or vice and versus, so to speak? It couldn't have been about Zamper, could it? She wasn't jealous of you, was she?"

"No, and it's none of your damned business," she snapped.

"I'll make a note of that, Betty. Understand, you don't have to talk, nor do you have to answer questions, but we can put you in the clink and hold you there for years as a material witness if we want to, can't we, Rocky?"

"Sure, if you want to," he agreed. "Should I take her now?"

Betty pulled away. "I say to hell with you and your clink! I didn't have to stick a knife into Zara to kill her. I have other means to kill off people I don't like. It takes a little longer but it lasts; they stay dead, and I can watch them suffer. That goes for writers too," she said.

"Don't try to intimidate an officer of the law," Rocky warned with surprising accuracy.

"And don't try to scare me," she sniffed.

"Going to tell me, Betty?" I asked again.

"No."

"Let me put her away," Rocky begged. There was a light dancing in his eyes.

"Not now," I said.

She snorted loudly at Rocky and left the room. She was such a charming girl—some day, I promised myself, I'd commit the perfect crime, and Potter would be the victim. In the meantime I knew I'd have to marry Vicky as quickly as possible if I wanted her to have even a shred of reputation left. I grinned at the thought. It wasn't difficult to take that resolve. Then I wondered. Perhaps Vicky would rather have a blasted reputation than me. No, she had said she would marry me. I looked over to see what she had been doing during the Potter conference. Her pad was filled with line drawings of cats.

CHAPTER ELEVEN

ROCKY BROKE INTO my pleasant musings with a cheery, "Well, Chief—who do you want me to arrest?"

"Nobody yet," I replied, "but I'd like you to get the Zamper fellow—and, Rocky, make sure he isn't armed."

"Okay," he agreed. He was a cheerful cuss and seemed tireless as he trotted away.

I leaned back and gave a deep sigh. All this cross-examining was beginning to get me down.

Vicky yawned sleepily. "This is a rum murder. Aren't we ever going to get any sleep?" She opened a compact and gave a few dabs on the end of the nose.

"Cheer up, sweetheart," I said as I pushed the powder away. "It will probably get worse, maybe a few more before we're through with it."

"Are you kidding?" She looked at me from the corner of her eye.

"Far from it. As a matter of fact, 'most anything can happen, and soon," I warned.

"What sort of things, Dean?" she asked anxiously.

"Attempts to cover up. We're here on a yacht, the murderer knows and we know he can't get away. We've been questioning the suspects. While we have nothing very tangible as yet, we do have a few facts and our information is growing. I have a theory. As our information piles up, the uncertainty and discomfort of the murderer will increase. I'm hoping he will be driven to do something, perhaps desperate, just to make sure his trail is covered."

"Do you mean to say you are trying to egg him on to do another murder? That's rotten, Dean!"

"Not necessarily another murder. I hope not. This case is practically tight. It isn't one of those affairs where clues lead to results. It's a case for deduction. We'll learn all we can about everybody and then figure it out. You can be sure of this, however, the person who owned the knife did not kill Zara."

Then you don't think Sarakov killed her?" she asked.

"No. The knife was stolen."

"What makes you so sure of that?"

"If Sarakov had anything to hide he would not have admitted that the knife was his, would he?"

"No, I suppose not. It's just like the one I bought. I meant to show it to you when I went back to the cabin."

"Why didn't you?"

"Because it wasn't there, Dean. It had been stolen."

"What!" I gasped. "Your knife . . ."

"There's no point to your excitement. You know I didn't kill her," she said.

"But this changes everything!" I insisted. "Shows how smart the murderer was. He didn't leave a single clue and he must have known there would be many suspects."

"And you're hoping he'll stop being smart, aren't you?"

"I hope he'll become nervous, worried, begin to wonder, feel insecure, be afraid that he has left some trail behind him. If he does that, we'll get him," I promised but not with too much conviction.

"Do you think maybe he'll try to get you?" She looked at me anxiously.

"I don't know. If they start tossing any more poisoned knives about I'll begin to think that someone doesn't like my Mandarin robe," I answered, trying to hide my concern.

"I don't, for one—it gives people the wrong impression. Besides, it hides the hair on your chest. Who gave you the darn thing, anyway?"

"A little fairy in the bottom of my garden. But seriously, it was a present from Shang."

"From Shang! I suppose he picked it out himself," she scoffed.

"That's exactly what happened. We were snooping through a store on Hollywood Boulevard one day. The proprietor suddenly let out a howl. I looked down and found Shang in the midst of autographing this very robe. Well, there was nothing else for me to do but buy it. It was too large for Shang, so he gave it to me."

Vicky gave her merry laugh and blew me a kiss.

"You win, my darling," she said. "But, in the future, I'll do all the picking for this family."

At that moment Rocky arrived with our next victim. It was the first opportunity I'd had to get a good look at the man. He was small—about five feet three, but powerfully built. He wore his black hair in a slick pompadour; his complexion was sallow and pockmarked; his eyes were beady and set too close together. Rocky showed him to a chair opposite me. I waded in immediately.

"Mr. Zamper—as you know, we're trying to get to the bottom of this unfortunate affair. There are a few questions I want to ask you, and I feel sure that I can count on your cooperation."

He inclined his head and blew a cloud of cigarette smoke through his nostrils.

"I shall be only too happy to help you." He spoke deliberately.

"That's splendid, Mr. Zamper. You were a fairly close friend of Zara—weren't you?"

He studied the tip of his cigarette a moment before replying. "I saw a good deal of her—if that's what you mean?"

"When did this friendship start?"

"About ten months ago. I'm an importer. She was furnishing an apartment. I sold her a number of rugs and tapestries. She was also very fond of Oriental jewelry and placed a standing order with me for something new every week."

"I see—that'd account for your going to see her once a week, of course, but according to reports you called more frequently."

"Oh, she discovered that I spoke Russian—which was her native tongue. I often used to spend the evening in her apartment and we would discuss—in Russian — Oriental art, a subject that amounted to a passion with her."

The man was far too glib with his answers to suit me.

"Did she ever talk about her past—before she came to this country?" I asked.

There was an almost imperceptible tightening of the muscles in his jaw. "No—she never spoke of that," he said tersely.

"And you weren't curious?"

"Perhaps—but in my business one is very careful not to offend a good customer by foolish curiosity."

"Of course, I can see that you're a good business man. Where were you in the line-up just before the Rajah threw the rubies into the water?"

"I was between Miss Ravelle and Mr. Sarakov."

"And after you dove—did you notice anything that might be construed as menacing to Zara?"

"No—I was intent on finding a ruby. I was lucky enough to get one, but I noticed nothing unusual. As you probably know—it is impossible to see very much under water."

The fellow should have been a lawyer—he knew all the answers, but he'd made one slip and would probably make more.

"Mr. Zamper, would you mind telling me why you argued with Zara earlier in the evening? I mean the argument that Sarakov interrupted."

He took time out to light a fresh cigarette. He gave a short laugh.

"Let me congratulate you, Mr. Mallory—you are well informed." He paused while I bowed. "The argument you refer to occurred because I told her that she should not have accepted the pearls from the Rajah —I said it would have been better publicity if she had refused the gift."

The chap was lying beautifully. I pushed a pencil and paper over to him.

"Would you mind writing your name and address

down?"

He smiled and shook his head. "I'm sorry. I was born in the utmost poverty and have never learned to write—a friend conducts all my correspondence for me."

Very clever—the friend was probably Julma Desa. I decided to let it pass for the moment.

"What do you know about Mr. Sarakov?"

"Not a great deal, I'm afraid. I have met him a few times at Zara's apartment—that is all."

"What were his relations with the dead girl?"

"I don't know. She seemed a little afraid of him."

"In what way?"

"Just that she appeared very subdued in his presence —like a child before a stern father."

"And this subdued role was unusual for her?"

He smiled wryly. "Very."

"Then you definitely think she was afraid of him?"

"He had some hold over her. He was the only man who could control her when she flew into a rage. It was more like hypnotism. I've seen her grovel before him."

"One more thing, Mr. Zamper. D'you know anything about curare?"

As I asked the question he emitted a dense cloud of smoke—masking his features. Whatever reaction his face had shown to my question had disappeared by the time the smoke had thinned away.

"I believe it is a poison," he answered cautiously.

"Have you ever seen any?"

He shook his head.

That settled it. It was time to cut out the fencing and get down to brass tacks. I was determined to show no quarter.

"Mr. Zamper, for the past few minutes we've been having a lot of fun—now I'm tired of playing."

His hands tightened on the edge of the table.

"I'm afraid I don't understand," he said.

Then I'll enlighten you. To begin, you've been importing curare and selling it to Sarakov." His lower jaw went slack, perspiration beads appeared on his forehead. "Also, you knew that the Rajah's real name was Julma Desa, that he was hired by Sid Tricker to play the role of a rajah. You knew all this because you live in the same house with him. Also, you knew the necklace the Rajah gave to Zara was a fake as were the rubies. We will now make a fresh start, Mr. Zamper."

All the suaveness and cocksureness had left him— he was in a tough spot and knew it. I felt soon he would be ready to answer my questions truthfully.

"We will begin by having you tell us about the slave market at Teheran." He did not answer, just stared sullenly at the table. "Come, Mr. Zamper, you answered readily enough before. I want you to tell me the part about Zara's past that you found so profitable for blackmail. You did approach Betty Potter, I know."

I guess he realized his game was up. He took a deep breath, leaned back in his chair and looked relieved.

"Yes, what you say is true. I met Zara first about four years ago in Teheran, Persia. I had a little money and when I saw her in the slave market I bought her. She was seventeen then. We lived there for a year before I took her to Vladivostok. I lost my money shortly after that, so I gave her her freedom. Some months later I ran into her in a dive in Shanghai—making a living as best she could. At the time, Shanghai was filled with Russian girls—girls who had fled to China after the defeat of the White Army—forced into the life they were leading to avoid starvation. A few days later I boarded a cargo boat and worked my way to America. I came to Hollywood and made a little money working as an extra. It was during this time that I met Julma Desa and rented a room in his house. Later I began importing rugs and jewelry which I sold around the studios. About ten months ago I saw Zara's picture in the paper, with the announcement that she had been signed for a long-term contract by Sid Tricker. I went to see her immediately." He paused and lit another cigarette.

"Was she glad to see you?" I asked.

He smiled. "Hardly—but she had to make the best of it."

"And a little later you decided the knowledge you had of her past was worth cash, isn't that right?"

He paled a little. "I had got into some trouble and needed money."

"What sort of trouble?"

"A woman," he answered glibly.

"Won't do, Zamper—at the time you got the ten thousand form her you purchased a high-powered limousine and hired a chauffeur."

He was surprised that I should know all this.

"You know a great deal, Mr. Mallory. My only excuse is that I wanted you to think that I was forced to demand money from her."

I smiled at his frankness. "You were supposed to get ten thousand more tonight, weren't you? Was that why you were arguing with her?"

"Yes. She said she would give it to me after the party and I didn't want to wait."

"And what did you need it for this time?"

"It was to have been the last. I was intending to sail for China—one can live a long time there on ten thousand dollars."

"What made you decide to leave a profitable place like Hollywood?"

"I received a visit from the immigration authorities. It seems that I neglected certain formalities on entering the country."

I smiled—then said quickly, "Curare was used to kill Zara."

Again that puff of smoke masked his features. I was sure the rat was doing it to cover up, but he surprised me at once.

"I know it," he said as the smoke cleared away. "I saw her body, the wound, the horrible smile on her face. I knew then but I didn't want to connect myself with the crime in any way. Didn't want to make you suspicious of me, but since you know so much about curare and its uses, why pick on me? There are others who know how to use it."

He was referring to Sarakov and Desa, of course.

"Knowing as you did that the rubies were fakes—why did you dive after them?"

"For the fun of it—I enjoy diving."

"Just for pleasure, eh? When did you first know they were going to have this diving stunt?"

"About a week ago. I was delivering a rug to Mr. Waetjen's house. He told me about it—he always liked to brag to me about his publicity stunts. I think he was a little jealous because Tricker took all the credit. He asked me to keep quiet about it."

"And did you?"

"I told Sarakov and Miss Ravelle—they were good customers of mine, so I tipped them off."

"How did you manage to get an invitation to this party?"

"Zara got it for me."

"Why?"

"Perhaps she wanted a friend she could trust somewhere near her," he suggested with brass—plenty of it.

"Well, Zamper, you're in a tough spot. It looks to me as if you'd planned the murder ahead of time; that Zara refused to give you the ten thousand dollars, so you decided to go through with the murder as planned. Later you intended getting the money from her cabin."

That definitely got a rise out of him. He jumped to his feet and shouted wildly, "NO! NO! NO! That is a lie! Why should I kill her—she had not got the money at the time I talked to her. If she were dead I would gain nothing."

That sounded logical—particularly since he knew she did not have the money in her possession.

"Are you sure she did not have the money?"

"Yes. She would not lie about that."

"What makes you so sure?"

"She knew what I intended to do. She was afraid."

"That you'd kill her?" I demanded quickly.

"No, of my plan to expose her."

"To whom?"

"Hollywood," he replied with a nasty grin.

That was another name for Betty and not fair to Hollywood.

"Do you know who was to supply the money?"

"No, I didn't ask her where it came from—I imagined it was an advance on her salary, that Sid was going to give it to her."

That sounded a little flimsy. I couldn't picture a man of his nefarious abilities not knowing the source of the gold supply. Anyway, it didn't matter much.

I went back to him. Mr. Zamper, do you know of anyone besides Sarakov with whom Zara had had trouble?"

He thought for a moment, then said, "About a week ago I went to her apartment. The maid let me in and showed me into the living-room. While I was waiting I heard a scuffle and a man's voice raised in anger. A moment later the bedroom door opened and Frank Lane came out—there was an angry welt across his face. He walked right past me without saying a word. Zara was in a bad temper when I saw her. She said, 'Zamper, you're a dirty little crook but I'd rather put up with you than some of the other people I know.'"

I decided I had all the information I wanted from him for the moment. I'd have put him under arrest, charged with murder but for the fact that, at present, I couldn't see what he had to gain by her death— instead, it looked as if he had everything to lose. He was too calculating a man to kill the goose that laid the golden eggs.

He was anxious to get away, knew that I was through with him for the moment. He rose and moved toward the door.

"Did you sell the story of Zara's life?" I threw at him.

He turned as though stung, looked at me with unbelieving eyes.

"Did you?" I demanded.

"I—I had made arrangements; she knew it. I had to do it to be sure of the money. Now, it makes no difference," he regretted. "She is dead."

"How long had she been a spy?" I asked.

He laughed. "A spy, Zara! You let thoughts of Mata Hari influence your judgment."

He turned and left hurriedly, like a man pursued by an angry dog.

"That is a first-class liar," I said.

"Lower than that," Vicky insisted.

"Want me to arrest him?" Rocky asked hopefully.

I shook my head. For a moment I thought I had loosened something in my ears because of the rumbling I heard. It was, however, nothing as simple as that but a babble of voices from outside, a rising crescendo of tongues, and then the door burst open and our suspects stormed into the room.

CHAPTER TWELVE

IT WAS A MOB SCENE in embryo; all the elements of hate, fear and suspicion were on their faces, indignation too, with grim determination.

They were led by Sarakov and Betty Potter. Zamper had joined their ranks, hung in the rear. I didn't like the look in Betty's eyes as she turned them on Vicky, nor did I relish the set fanatical stare on Sarakov's face as he marched across the room.

The crowd was against us, we were greatly outnumbered. I saw Rocky's great paw go to the holster on his hip. He realized what their anger meant to us, was prepared for it and I was glad. I was also sure that Betty Potter, that sweet little bitch, had turned the trick.

There was no nonsense about Rocky as he squared off to face the crew, putting himself between them and us. His jaw was set and his eyes gleamed as he asked, "Well, what do you think you want?" He looked them over beginning with Sarakov. Even that giant stopped and seemed a trifle confused. When Rocky spotted Zamper he boomed, "Who in hell let you in, and why?"

Zamper, who had tagged along in the rear, had not expected any such reception. He seemed a little confused and turned to look behind him.

"I did," Betty announced. "You've no right to treat us the way you have just because he says so." She pointed disdainfully at me.

Rocky strode up to and towered over her. "Now, you listen to me, you cheap little gossip-mongering, news-weasel—another word out of you and you know where'll you go, right back into the can." He reached for her, but with a squeal Betty backed away.

I cheered Rocky—and was Betty's face red! When she was out of reach of his long arm she threatened, "I'll have you broken for this, my man!"

"Swell, I've been wanting to go fishing and all I've needed was the time. Go ahead!" He returned his attention to the others, "Get out, all of you!"

"Just a minute, Rocky," I said. "Let them talk, that's what they came in to do."

"All right. Say it and be quick," he ordered.

"Miss Potter came to me, presented some facts, made them seem plausible," Sarakov began. "I agreed with her. Since this is supposed to be a free country I think we have a right to be heard."

Rocky's good old jaw shot out. "Are you a citizen of the United States?" he demanded.

Sarakov was startled. "Why, no, I'm not."

"Then let someone who is talk. There are too many foreigners sticking their noses into our business, trying to ruin our country, undermining our democracy, talking about our Bill of Rights, our freedom which they abuse and try to destroy like the lousy termites they are."

"I demand . . ." Sarakov shouted after a moment's pause, shouted with a technique learned from certain subversive groups.

"Quiet!" Rocky boomed over him. "I'll listen to you later. Come here, trouble!" He beckoned to Betty. "Since you started this little party suppose you tell us what it's all about." He squared off and waited for her to speak.

"You've let this man make a fool out of you," she began. "I don't know why you listened to him in the first place."

"That's my business," he replied. "Go on!"

"Well, he's been very smart. He fooled you and he fooled us until I began to put two and two together."

"You're developing," I said with a smile. "You usually devote your time to one and one."

"It was that which gave me the clue," she retorted. She turned to Rocky. "Now, you listen to me and get this straight as I tell it to you. This man and his friend are just as much to be suspected as any of us, perhaps more so."

Of all the things I had expected from Betty, an accusation against either Vicky or myself was the last. "Why, you . . ." I was ready to have a go at her but both Vicky and Rocky stopped me.

She put a restraining hand on my arm and Rocky scowled before he said, "Just a minute, Mr. Mallory, I'm taking over for the moment. Talk, Miss Potter!"

She did, by the yard. When given a free rein Betty Potter has no equal.

"He hoodwinked you," she charged, "because he had plenty to hide. He's been having an affair with Zara!"

"Who told you?" I asked, trying to be flippant but I knew it was no use. Every last person in the group would believe her. St. Denis and Naomi had intimated it earlier and I knew before she raced on that it was going to look like hell and believable before she got through. How could I explain to them that Zara was not my type, particularly when other men were willing to sell their souls for her favors? How could I tell them that she had been furious because I didn't fall for her stuff? I wasn't going to tell them and wouldn't. Zara had been furious with me many times because I had never once made a pass at her. She had tried to get me, she believed any man could be had. She had even suggested that I was not regular. Why, earlier in the evening she had tried again. It had been like that at each story conference we had had. She had been smart, had set the stage; had done just about everything a woman could do and I had enjoyed blocking her, partly out of devilishness but particularly because her lack of finesse made her repulsive to me.

"Everybody on the Tricker lot knew about it," Betty went on. "They also know that you've been playing a double game, that Vicky had been sore at Zara because of your affair, and at you too," she added for emphasis.

She faced up to Rocky. "Yesterday on the lot Vicky Blaire and Zara had a scrap. They were stopped just before they began to pull hair. Deny it, if you can," she challenged Vicky.

"Why should I?" Vicky demanded.

"And you were heard to say that you would fix her if it was the last thing you ever did," Betty went on. "Didn't you?"

"I did," Vicky agreed. "Like you, Betty, I have ways of doing things. Don't forget I was designing the costumes for the *Blue Lagoon*. I'll have to change all my plans now, since someone decent will play the part."

"Vicky, were you going to do a thing like that to me?" Sid asked sorrowfully.

"Sure, Sid. You wouldn't have known the difference," she replied.

Betty had lost the spotlight for the moment but she directed the attention back to herself. "Never mind, Sid. She won't do anything more to you when we get through with her.

"Do you know how Zara was killed?" she asked Rocky.

He nodded.

"Then I'll tell you who did it. She did." She pointed at Vicky.

The woman was clean off her nut making an accusation like that or else she had something up her sleeve that was going to make it look pretty dark for Vicky and probably me.

"That's a serious charge, you know," Rocky warned.

"I know it, all right, but I know when she did it, and how she did it," Betty boasted.

"Suppose you tell us all about it," I suggested. "And why don't you sit down," I invited the others. "If I know Betty she'll talk for an hour. She gets paid so much a word and she's accustomed to being long-winded."

They followed my suggestion. Sarakov and Zamper sat at the table opposite us. Desa, still dressed as he had been earlier in the evening, sat on the end of the table. My pad and pencil were still there. Sarakov pushed them out of his way. Betty stood facing us. Sid was beside her. Grey and Lane were at the far end of the table. Naomi and St. Denis stood together. I found myself thinking that they almost made a jury. No one had ever faced a tougher group. Rocky, Vicky and I had delved into their pasts, had turned up some ugly facts. They were not going to be too lenient with us and Betty knew it.

"Vicky Blaire brought fishing equipment with her," Betty started.

"The knife," I thought.

"New equipment, hooks, lines, leaders, sinkers, everything, including a knife."

Rocky looked toward Vicky in amazement. She doesn't look like a woman who would go in for fishing but she's good at it. I know because we had fished around the Island many times. She can outcast me and can handle a tuna or a yellowtail better than I can.

Betty had seen that look of Rocky's, had seen Vicky's slight inclination of her head and relished it.

"Vicky Blaire was away from the boat a little while before the murder. Oh, she has an excuse because she brought him and his crazy clothes with her," she added.

Shang woke up suddenly and barked.

"And his dog," Betty added. "Very nice trick it was too. They were pretty much by themselves after they came aboard. I happened to see something in her cabin, something which I misread at the moment. I won't go into that."

"Go ahead," Vicky suggested. "That's tame compared to the line you're pulling now."

"Well, if you want the world to know it. I saw them coming out of her cabin and her dress lay in a heap on the floor. But it wasn't what one would think, I see it now. She had been overboard trying her plan. He had been covering for her. They are both in it together. This sort of thing is easy for his disordered mind which spends its time thinking of ways to kill people."

"I haven't found a good one for you yet," I said.

"You heard him." She included them all. "You heard him threaten my life. He's doing all this to distract our attention."

"You're balmy, Betty," I said. "Your trumped-up little story doesn't hold together."

"Oh, doesn't it?" she cried. "How about this?" She plunked down a knife scabbard and a small tin ointment-box.

Then, Vicky's knife had been used and the tin box probably held curare.

"I found them in Vicky's cabin," Betty stated, "along with a wet bathing suit."

Vicky's eyes spouted fire. "You had a lot of nerve!" she said.

"Are those things yours or not?" Betty demanded.

"The knife case looks like mine, all right, but I never saw the box before. Where is my knife?"

"You know where it is. It killed Zara!" Betty shouted.

"Who knew you had fishing equipment with you?" I asked when the tumult had died down.

"Why, Dean!" She gazed at me wide-eyed. "Do you think . . ."

"No! Good God, no! But these people!" I didn't realize that I was shouting. "Listen, Vicky, someone must have known about your stuff. Who did?"

"Just about everybody in this room except you and Rocky," she replied. "You see, when we were at the dock waiting to get aboard, one of the deck hands was taking care of the bags. My bag had to be the one he dropped. It popped open and out went all my stuff. They all saw it because it was strewn all over the pier."

I sighed with relief and lit a cigarette. As I flicked the match out I realized that Zamper had been writing something on my pad. I reached forward to drop the match in a tray and saw upside down, "Vicky Blaire is the murderer."

They were all looking at Rocky, waiting for him to say something.

"Thanks very much for the information," he said. "We'll carry on as we have been doing until the fog lifts and the sheriff gets here."

"Do you mean to say you're not going to arrest her?" Betty gasped.

"I'm not arresting any of you at the moment. Mr. Mallory hasn't advised it."

"Of course he wouldn't advise your arresting her," she sneered.

"I'm assuming that responsibility myself," Rocky replied. "There's more against some of the rest of you, better motives and certainly more telling information. So why don't you just go to bed and sleep a little."

He turned his back on them and said, "How about some coffee, Mallory, or isn't it time yet?"

"Sounds good to me," Vicky agreed, "and thanks, Rocky."

"Just a moment, Rocky. Don't let them leave here, any of them, not yet."

"Just try to keep us here!" Betty stormed.

"Do you want to be gagged?" Rocky asked. "You're the kind of a dame who makes bachelors out of good men. Shut up and give someone else a chance for a while. What is it, Mallory?"

"I've a few things to say to these people and I want them kept here for a little while. I want to do some snooping myself."

"Don't you dare go to my cabin without . . ." Betty shrilled.

"Your secrets are safe with me, or are they?" I asked pointedly.

"Oh!" she gasped. "How you'll pay for all this!"

"Remember it's the woman who pays, and pays, and pays," I jeered. I ignored her after that and spoke to the others. "I know how you must feel about this and I don't blame you. It's unfortunate that we must all be suspects. Even Miss Potter has something to hide. She was trying to buy the story of Zara's life from Zamper. Zamper in turn was blackmailing Zara and holding Betty over her head, load though it seems."

"It's a lie," Betty cried.

"Prove it, later," I added and went on. "Zara slapped Miss Potter's face earlier this evening. You'll admire the dead girl for her courage—we've all wanted to do the same thing many times.

"Zara was a natural trouble-maker. I believe she was either a spy or was connected with a spy ring. She had in her possession a valuable paper, a plan which she intended to sell to enemies of this country. We have enemies, you know, many people who are supposed to be our friends are trying to destroy our nation to set up something which will be so much worse than anything we have ever known—but we haven't time to go into political theory now.

"I want you all to realize the entire situation. I am willing for you to know what I know—perhaps someone of you will want to help me. I may be wrong, there may be no international significance connected with her death, it may be just plain hatred. Of one thing I am certain, her death was planned."

"What makes you so sure of that?" Sid asked.

"The facts. Zamper knew about the diving stunt in advance."

"What if I did?" Zamper demanded. "I did not kill her."

"Nor am I accusing you." I paused. "But you did know about the diving stunt, didn't you?"

"Sure. I told Sarakov and Naomi Ravelle.

Desa knew, we talked about it."

"But Desa was not in the water," I said. Desa gave me a relieved glance.

"Nor was Miss Blaire," I added with a look toward Betty.

"We have your word for it, yours alone," she cried. "She could have slipped over the other side, could have been waiting for Zara to dive into the water."

"She was tied to me at the time."

"That is true," Desa stated. "I saw the rope, she was

not in the water."

"Then Vicky Blaire cut Zara's leg as she left the deck," Betty insisted.

"It's a nice idea, Betty, but I won't refute it now. We have rather conclusive proof that Zara was stabbed under the water. That, however, is beside the point."

"Just what is the point?" Sarakov asked.

"Desa brought some curare into this country, sold it to Zamper, who in turn sold or gave it to others. Sarakov, you used curare. Naomi Ravelle knew about it and its use, others of you could have known. Every one of us had reason to wish Zara dead," I stated.

"Don't say that, Dean," Sid begged.

"It's true, Sid. Even you."

His eyes begged me not to divulge his secret. Betty's mouth, eyes and ears were open hopefully. Naomi looked positively ill; St. Denis squirmed uncomfortably, but I had no intention of giving their secrets away.

"Mr. Grey, Mr. Lane, St. Denis, and even I, had no particular love for the young lady," I said.

I saw Grey's eyes close. He had loved her.

"So what do you get when you add it up?" Betty asked.

"That one of you killed Zara. Figure it out. That's what we're trying to do. And now, Rocky, if you will keep these good people here for a little while, we'll do a little hunting."

I took Vicky by the arm and led her outside.

"Why did you tell them all those things?" she asked.

"Let them suspect and fight among themselves."

"And make the murderer feel less secure, is that it?" she asked.

'That hits it right on the nose," I replied. "Now for a little exploring."

CHAPTER THIRTEEN

OUR SEARCH HAD netted us very little. We had found a box of curare in Desa's cabin but it had not been touched, was quite intact. There was also a beautiful pair of red morocco slippers with a card in them. A present from Zamper.

In Zamper's cabin we found an envelope between the spring and mattress. It contained a few pages, hastily written, about Zara, giving her origin and brief facts of her early life.

There was some curarine in Sarakov's cabin, a small box of it. His cabin was orderly and neat. His bath too was neatness itself. Even his soiled towels were hung along the shower rail instead of in a heap on the floor as they so often are.

"Didn't do you much good, this search, did it?" Vicky asked.

"It will, I think, have a great psychological value," I said. "The murderer will be wondering what I found, if anything."

"I like Sarakov," she said unexpectedly. "I like neat men. His towels looked as if he had washed them out and hung them up to dry."

"I'll remember that and buy you a washing-machine," I promised.

"I may work to support you," she said, "but it won't be in the laundry business."

We went back to the lounge.

"I suppose we can go," Betty sneered.

"The quicker the better," I replied.

She wheeled away. I reached across the table and took the top sheet of paper. "Thought you couldn't write, Zamper," I said. "Now, I know who threatened Zara. The writing was the same as the one on the note Shang found."

"What?" Sarakov boomed.

"Nothing, just a little secret between Zamper and me."

Zamper was scowling at me and cowering before Sarakov.

"You're quite a boy, Zamper," I said. "You had several irons in the fire. Don't try to pull any chestnuts out, however, of any kind, or if you have tried you'd better put them back, maybe ten of them, understand?"

He stalked out of the room. The others followed, all but Grey, who demanded, "Do you mean to say that you think he has my money and you're letting him walk out of here?"

Betty's curiosity had held her in the door. "Did you lose some money?" she cooed.

"That will be all," I said, dismissing them both.

I saw her link her arm in Grey's, could almost hear her pumping him in her best gushalistic manner.

"Why didn't you let me search the egg?" Rocky demanded.

"Better this way, I think," I answered.

We talked for perhaps ten minutes, or rather they asked me questions which I tried to answer. It helped to clarify my mind. Frankly I was stumped. In a story I see to it that there are clues planted along the trail, like the game of Hare and Hound. I had clues, all right, but I didn't like 'em. Zara had been killed with either Sarakov's or Vicky's knife. There was some confusion there. Curare had been put in Vicky's cabin. That was a plant and the sort of thing that anyone might have done.

They realized that I wanted to think, and for a long while they were quiet. Shang came and sat in my lap. I stroked his back while I thought of all the things still left to be done. There were more things I wanted to know. Why had Frank and Zara quarreled in her home? What was he doing there anyhow? And what about Sid? In fact, what about everything?

Vicky leaned over and looked at my wristwatch—it

was two thirty-five.

"Listen, Sherlock—before I'll go through any more cross-examination—I'm going to eat."

She reached for Shang, put him on the table and stood up stiffly. I suddenly realized that I was feeling pretty famished myself.

"That's a swell idea, precious—let's go!" I said.

She picked up Shang and we were on our way. Rocky too liked the idea; he was holding the door open for us.

"Lead us to the galley—we crave food," Vicky said.

"I could do with a few hams myself," he replied hungrily.

I craved fresh air. We paused on the deck. The air was fresh, all right, and soggy. It went right through my Mandarin robe and hit me all over. I shivered.

"Got the creeps?" Vicky asked.

"No. Just cold shivers!" My teeth were about to clatter.

"It's a good thing it's foggy or you'd be out cold," she said cheerfully. "Remember the knife and, unless I'm wrong, you're in for something more."

That gave me a real chill, of apprehension. I might be in danger but because she had been with me all through the investigation she too was in danger. I cursed myself for being a fool. Only a sap so busy with a sense of his own importance would have done a thing like that. I said nothing about it, however. I'd just have to be on my toes to protect us both.

"The fog's with us," Rocky said. "We're getting the breaks on this case, all right. Nothing will put in here until daylight, if then."

I went to the rail and peered toward the shore.

"What are you looking for?" he asked.

"The lights from the shore," I replied.

"Over the other side. The fog's got you confused."

"It isn't the fog, Rocky, my boy," Vicky jeered. "The master mind is up a tree."

"And where is the *Parrakeet*, my boat?" I asked,

ignoring her crack.

"Where you left it, if you had a good anchor," he replied.

There was a milkiness to the fog, owing to the moon, which I supposed still did its silver shining above the fog-bank. We groped along the deck. We passed a cabin. I was tempted to peer in at the window. It was Naomi's.

The shade was down, but not quite far enough. St Denis was with her—from what I could see everything was hunky-dory between them. Vicky took one peek and said, "Oh!"

Rocky led us through one end of the saloon toward the galley. Most of the guests who were to have spent the night at the hotel seemed to be there. Some were lying on the red velour seats that lined the walls— others were either playing bridge or talking in little groups. A more bored and jaded collection of people who'd been places would be hard to duplicate—even among the ultra-sophisticates of Beverly.

Quite accidentally I stepped on a stomach—it belonged to a beautiful creature who, I should judge, was fast approaching the mighty age of nineteen.

She opened a pair of languorous eyes and, in a Hollywood interpretation of the Bond Street drawl, said, "Won't you *pleeze* watch where you're putting your big feet—that was my stomach; do I need a Keep Off sign?"

I told her I was very sorry and would try to remember to detour next time. The cavalcade pushed on and entered the galley. It was empty—the chef had probably gone to bed hours ago.

On his previous trip to the galley Rocky had made the most of his time—he knew where everything was kept. He took some plates out of a locker, glasses and knives and forks. Next he opened a large door at the far end of the narrow room. Out staggered a weird spectacle.

It was Betty Potter, her face blue with cold. In one hand she clutched half a chicken, in the other a bottle of champagne. It was a lucky thing for her that we'd arrived—after all, a cold-storage room is a bad place to park.

"Da-damn d-door cl-closed on me," she chattered.

Her teeth were clicking. I spotted a half-empty bottle of cooking brandy on a shelf. I poured about four fingers and held it to her lips. She gulped it down, coughed, sputtered, glowered at me, but the shivers disappeared.

"You should have moved about to keep yourself warm," I said.

"How can you keep warm in an ice-house, dope?" she returned.

I let that pass and went back to the door of the refrigerator room, opened it, left it on the latch, played with it, gave it a slight push but nothing happened. That door didn't close of its own accord. It had been pushed shut. I wondered just how many people on the boat outside of myself would like to be rid of Betty. She gives me a pain where I sit down but . . . No, definitely, Betty in some way was not desirable to the murderer. I couldn't imagine anyone else doing a thing like that. A person would have to be desperate to try that sort of murder.

"The door didn't close, Betty darling. It was pushed shut," I said, "by someone who loves you very much."

"Why, the lousy . . ."

"Never mind the headlines. What do you know about this murder?"

"Not a damn thing and you won't tell me," she complained.

"But the murderer thinks you know something, is sure you do. Think if you can, will you, and tell us what it is?"

She was honestly puzzled. I could see her brain begin to work. "I don't know, Dean," she said.

"Okay. Perhaps it will come to you. Remember this, stay in your cabin and keep your door locked. I told you that before," I said with mock severity.

"I suppose you'd like me to starve to death," she snapped.

The thought was not unpleasant but I didn't elaborate on it. Instead I said, "Betty—I'm surprised at you. We've always been such pals. Now be a good girl and run along to your cabin and while you tear that chicken apart— think about what it is that you know, and shouldn't. I mean about the murder," I added quickly. I didn't want her to have brain fever until the case was over.

At the door she turned—Betty could never leave any place quietly, she always had to make at least one parting crack. "Oh, Mr. Mallory—you'll probably be interested in knowing that I'm wiring the cutest thing for my column. It's all about a torn white dress." To that announcement she added a dirty little smile and left.

"She should have frozen to death," I said.

Vicky patted me on the shoulder and said not to mind.

"Here we are, Boss!" Rocky called.

He had emerged from the cold-storage room. In his arms he held three bottles of champagne and two hams. He unloaded his cargo on the table, then dug out a loaf of bread and some butter. One ham slid to the floor but we had plenty. There being no chairs we propped ourselves against the counters and tore into the food. Shang tried to carry off the fallen ham and kicked up one hell of a row when I suggested that it might be a little too much for him to tackle at one sitting. He finally allowed me to cut off a few hunks for him.

For a while we ate in silence—at least Vicky and I did. Rocky was busy with good thick slices, a bite of ham then a bite of bread. He'd slow up to pull the fat off and toss it to Shang. It was one way to have a ham sandwich and very effective if you like a thorough grease job. When the orgy was over I filled three glasses from the one remaining bottle. I raised my glass and said, "Henceforth—lips that touch liquor shall never touch mine."

Vicky gave me a funny look. "Have you gone nuts? What's the big idea?"

I put one arm around her.

"Angel child," I said, "when we've killed this drink I'm quitting."

She looked me straight in the eyes for a few seconds. "You—you really mean you're going on the wagon?"

"Will be—in about ten seconds."

Rocky grinned. "I hope you can make it." He picked up his glass.

We clinked glasses all around and raised our elbows, but before we drank Vicky said, "Don't swear off, Dean. Try, if you want to, but don't swear off. If you try and slip that's one thing, but if you give your word and don't keep it—" She slid from the table. "Well, I'm funny about my word or promises. I don't make them if I don't intend to keep them and—oh, nuts! Drink your damned fool head off if you want to." She perched herself on a table which looked like a butcher's block.

"Here's to a wise little lady," Rocky said. We drank.

She had made me think. I sat there preoccupied. She lifted Shang to the block beside me. He snuggled close. Rocky was an orderly soul. He cleared up the mess, stowed the empty bottles away, rinsed the glasses. Vicky found a towel and dried them.

I slid to my feet. I wanted to talk to Frank Lane. They followed me back to the saloon, which was just as we had left it. As we started across the end of the room I heard a shriek. Shang had forgotten to detour and had scampered across the Bond Street belly.

"My God!" she shrilled. "I thought it was a tarantula!"

Gingerly we stepped over her and went back to the deck.

"What gives?" Rocky asked.

"You can get Frank Lane."

He went off into the fog. We ambled back into the lounge and closed the door behind us.

Vicky paused during a powder job to ask, "How is it going, Maestro?"

"It isn't, Vicky."

"I could guess that," she said.

"I can pick three or four murderers out of the lot so far and we haven't tried Lane," I said.

She applied the last dab, snapped the lid shut. I moved over, slipped my arm about her waist.

"Worried?" she asked.

"About you. You may know too much, so no matter what happens keep mum. Will you promise me that?"

"Yes."

"I mean it, Vicky. At first I wasn't going to tell you my fears but, damn it all, I can't have anything happen to you, so forget you are a woman, lace up your lips and become a deaf mute for a while."

She grinned gloriously, reached up, kissed me, gave my hair a rumple.

"We're in it together," she said. "Partners."

I knew then if she married me it would always have to be partners or it would be no go. For one of the first times in my life I was a little afraid. Not of Vicky, nor marriage, but of my own ability to make a go of it.

CHAPTER FOURTEEN

ROCKY BROUGHT IN Frank Lane. He was looking a bit soured on the world—Frank Lane was I mean. He'd always been a sardonic sort of cuss, or so I'd always thought. I think he'd had a tough time in life. It was only lately that he'd got a break by directing for Sid. Prior to that he'd been eking out a precarious existence with the small independents, but he knew his job a whole lot better than some of the much-touted big-shot directors of the major studios. The thing I liked best about him was his ability to make a picture from a book and still have the original story recognizable. God knows it is a rare quality in dear old Hollywood. He sat down and gave me a questioning look.

"Go ahead and shoot, Dean—maybe we'll get some good dialogue out of it."

That crack had reference to *Black Lightning*—we'd had some difference of opinion over some of the dialogue I'd written. It all ended peacefully with Dean Mallory as top dog, so I could afford to be generous and allow him to get the odd crack in once in a while.

I smiled and said, "Maybe we can, Frank. I need a few good lines to explain a situation. Suppose you start off by telling me where you were when the diving stunt was on?"

"I was ready for a swim when the stunt was announced. It smelled so, I decided to wait. I went aft. I was leaning over the stern rail, smoking a cigarette and wondering how much longer the blasted party was going to last."

"Did anyone see you there?"

"I doubt it very much—they were all in the bow."

"How did you know it was a publicity stunt?"

He gave a dry laugh. "Did you ever see Sid connected

with anything that wasn't a publicity stunt of some kind?"

I was forced to agree with him there. "Nevertheless, that leaves me with only your word that you were where you say you were at the time Zara was murdered."

He gave me a disgusted look. "My suit was dry when I ran forward." He paused. "But I can't prove it, that's the hell of it."

"Maybe you can if necessary," I suggested.

"I hope so. It seems to me, in the case of a murder, there's usually a motive necessary. Perhaps you can supply me with one that'd give me sufficient reason for killing Zara."

"Had you ever quarreled with her?" I asked.

"I had as little conversation with that young lady as was possible."

"I take it that you mean you've had as little to do with her as possible since the time she slapped your face in the bedroom of her apartment?"

His face darkened. "So you've heard about that, eh? Well—suppose she did slap my face—what of it? People have been known to have their faces slapped in bedrooms without murder as a wind-up."

"I know, Frank, but I also know that unreturned love has often wound up in a murder."

He inhaled deeply on his cigarette before replying.

"All right, Dean—you're groping around trying to tie me into this murder. Now, I'll tell you why it's not only illogical, but absolutely ridiculous. In the first place, I've lived too long in this world, and have had too much experience to lose my head over a woman. If I wanted her and she couldn't see it that way . . ." He shrugged. "That would end it. You've been out here long enough to know that. Oh hell, Hollywood's no different from any other city where women are concerned. Also, as you're well aware, I've had a long tough pull in this picture game. *Black Lightning* was my first picture and it's going to be a success. I'm to direct *Blue Lagoon*. In other words, I intend to ride to the top of the heap on your stories. If you think I'm fool enough to run the risk of wrecking everything that I've struggled years to attain—then you're crazier than a supervisor."

This all sounded very logical, particularly since I knew that Lane didn't have the reputation of being a woman chaser.

"I'm inclined to agree with you, Frank. You've got too much sense to get everything in an uproar over a piece of foolishness. I'm willing to grant you all that —but I'd like to know what the trouble was between you and Zara."

He tightened up. "Sorry, old man—but I'm afraid you'll have to just take my word for it that there was nothing personal in our row. By that, I mean that I told the lady what I thought of her, which was her reason for slapping my face—but at no time have I had the slightest interest in her physically. She was a glorious-looking creature—with the disposition of a rattlesnake."

I'd known Frank long enough to know that he occasionally had some very goofy ideas, and that he was eccentric enough to stick to them—even if it got him into trouble. It began to look as if he'd gotten another one of them.

"Listen, Frank—there's no sense in making a horse's tiara out of yourself. I'm willing to believe that you did not commit the murder. Now you start throwing suspicion on yourself because you want to be secretive over the row you had with her. What's the matter—trying to shield someone?"

His eyes went cold. "That's my business, Flatfoot."

I gave up. I didn't like the way he said that either. After all, if a man deliberately tries to put his foot in it, that's his lookout.

"All right, Frank—you may go to your cabin. Thanks to your own stubbornness, you're still under suspicion. If you decide to talk later—I'll be glad to listen."

He favored me with another of his sardonic smiles— he got up and pushed off.

He was a peculiar mixture. Born of an English father and a Spanish mother, it seemed as if the two races were constantly at war within him. There'd been no particular point in questioning him about curare. I was fairly well satisfied in my mind that he hadn't committed the murder, and I couldn't quite picture a man swimming the length of a yacht underwater with a poisoned knife in his hand or mouth and then groping around trying to find his intended victim. But I did want to know about his row with Zara. The only possible explanation for his attitude was a desire to shield someone, someone he feared to be guilty. But whom? Not Zamper, surely. No one except possibly a woman would try to shield Zamper, and the only likely woman would be his mother. Nor would there be any reason, that I knew, why Lane would shield Sarakov. Could it be Sid?

I had to admit that was a possibility. Frank Lane was loyal. Sid had given him a chance, had taken him out of little time, had had faith in him and had made him a front-line director. Yes, he might do it for Sid. He had several reasons for shielding Sid. His loyalty and his desire to go on.

He wouldn't give a damn what happened to Betty Potter. Who would? As far as I knew he had no connection with Desa or Grey. That left Basil St. Denis and Naomi. He didn't like St. Denis, that was obvious in his direction. He made St. Denis act, which was a major miracle in itself, but Frank never relished the job, never worked with the warmth and understanding that he used when putting Naomi through her paces.

Naomi! They had always been warm friends. Then too he had been watching on deck when Zara and Naomi had had their quarrel. Perhaps because of that quarrel and other things he was shielding Naomi. I'd find out.

"I'm beginning to feel like a heel," Vicky said. "I'm glad you only write murder stories. Digging into people's lives is dirty business."

"And we're in it up to our necks," I reminded her.

I asked Rocky to bring Naomi in. "And," I added, "if she has company, leave it behind."

Vicky gave a deep sigh. "Why don't you leave her alone, Dean? I think she's a nice girl—even if she did kill Zara."

I said, "Because I've got to keep on, sorting these facts and motives. If I don't it will all come out in the papers."

"That wouldn't be so good," she said. "Keep going."

At that moment Rocky showed up with Naomi.

She was looking positively radiant, if a little worried. Evidently I'd been misjudging St. Denis. As soon as she sat down I asked, "What're you looking so happy about?"

She smiled and said, "Oh—nothing."

I cocked a querulous eye at her.

"Well, my dear, the next time you're doing nothing be sure that your shades are pulled all the way down."

She blushed furiously.

Then Vicky cut in, "Don't mind him, Naomi. He's got that kind of a mind, but—the part about the shades is darned good advice just the same."

"All right, Naomi—I apologize for the kidding. What I wanted to ask you was why you were so nervous when I questioned you before. Why?"

My kidding had been a bit too personal, but I'd accomplished what I'd started out to do—to get her flustered and consequently off guard.

By this time the poor kid had composed herself somewhat. She looked straight at me, shook her head and said, "Sorry, Dean—but that's something I can't tell you."

I was running into more stubbornness—then I got an idea.

"Now, Naomi, don't be foolish. I'm not even suspecting you in any way of being remotely connected with the murder—that's finished—I've got the murderer."

This statement took everyone by surprise. I could feel Vicky start beside me, Rocky's mouth popped open, while Naomi suddenly went deathly pale.

"Who—who is it?" she asked in a hushed voice, her

lovely dark eyes wide with terror.

"No reason why I should keep it a secret—it was Frank Lane."

Naomi immediately burst into tears. "No! No! It isn't true, I tell you it's impossible!"

I had not expected such an outburst. I had wanted to get to the crux of Frank Lane's stubbornness. I had.

At that moment Frank Lane stepped into the lounge. He walked swiftly to where we were sitting, gave one glance at the sobbing girl, then turned a furious face on me.

"God damn you, Dean! Leave the girl alone!" he thundered.

I thought he was going to leap at my throat. Rocky must have thought so too—he moved over close to him. "You're too damn dumb to solve this mystery in a million years, so I'll save you the trouble—I'm the murderer!"

"Father!" she cried.

The agonizing cry sprang from Naomi's lips. Instantly she was in his arms, sobbing. So that was it. I could see the resemblance now. Standing there with their cheeks pressed together, staring defiantly down at me, it was very marked. The underlying, basic structure of the two faces was the same, the shape and expression of the fine, dark eyes, the finely chiseled features and general carriage of the head. Funny I'd never noticed it before.

For a moment they held their tense pose, then I said, "Very well, Frank—suppose you tell your story?"

Fresh terror appeared in Naomi's eyes. She turned a pleading face to her father.

"No! It can't be true. Father—tell him you didn't do it!"

He shook his head sadly. "I'm sorry, little girl—but it's true."

Horror-stricken, she watched him take the chair she had just vacated. Rocky thoughtfully moved a comfortable one up for her. Frank Lane, with slow deliberation, lit a cigarette and took several long puffs on it, apparently in deep thought. Finally he leaned back and raised his eyes to mine.

"I may as well give you the whole story," he said. "You know now that Naomi's my daughter. I kept the fact a secret because I knew that one day I would get my big opportunity, and when that time came I intended to make a big star out of her. Naturally, if the fact was known that the girl I wished to star was my own daughter I would be accused of favoritism—regardless of her ability as an actress—and in consequence would run into a lot of trouble which might ruin her chances. My chance came, as you know, with Tricker Pictures and I chose Naomi to play the lead in my first big assignment—*Black Lightning*. Everyone agreed that she gave a marvelous performance. I felt that her future was assured. Then Zara came on the scene. I tried to talk Sid out of taking her on, but it was no use—Zara had him twisted around her little finger. When it came time to cast for *Blue Lagoon*, in spite of all my protests, the lead was given to Zara. In an endeavor to placate me, Sid gave Naomi a part in it. When Zara heard about that, she flew into a violent rage and crashed into Sid's office, saying that Naomi was too close to her type and that he'd have to put her out of the cast. Sid came to me and said that he'd decided that Naomi did not fit the part. We had quite a row over it.

"Of course, in the end, I gave in. If I lost the picture it would mean that I would not be able to help my daughter in the future. I would also be throwing away the opportunity that I'd worked years to get. A short time ago I heard, indirectly, that Zara was trying to get Sid to replace me with another director. I went at once to her apartment. She was in her bedroom having a massage. She admitted that what I'd heard was true and added that I was a lousy director anyway. I lost my temper and told her a lot of truths about herself. She sprang at me and slapped my face. I had just enough sense to leave before I lost control of myself completely."

He paused, lit another cigarette, then continued. "I took the matter up with Sid, but he denied that he was intending taking me off the picture. Last evening, however, he informed me that he was going to give the picture to Jules Rambeau. I knew that Zara was at the bottom of it and that if she were out of the way I would get the picture and my daughter would play the lead. I'd heard Sid and Waetjen talking over this publicity stunt. The walls of his office are very thin and it is possible to overhear conversations. My office was next to his. Consequently, I knew about the diving stunt in advance. I laid my plans, as I thought, carefully. When I saw Vicky's knife on the pier I knew how I'd do it and leave no trace behind. It was very simple really. I stole the knife, left the tin of curare in her cabin when she went to get you. When the diving started I was in the bow, but on the opposite side from the crowd. I noted that Zara was the only one in a white bathing suit and that she was nearest the bow. When the rubies were thrown I dove from the port side, swam around the bow underwater. I saw Zara below me groping around on the bottom. It was the work of a moment to swim down, gash her leg, and swim away. I came up on the port side. I'd previously dropped a rope over the rail. I climbed up, pulled the rope up after me and was at the rail by the time they were trying to free Zara."

I gave him a poker face and said, "You forgot to mention how you dried your shirt tail—that's very important, and what you did with the knife."

He bowed sarcastically. "Of course, I simply dropped the knife."

Naomi sat in a trance, staring at me, her eyes brimmed with tears. I could hear Vicky sniffling beside me. The whole thing was very unpleasant but I had to go through with it.

"Frank," I said, "I'm sorry to hear this, but you've told a very convincing tale. You admit that you had very good reasons for wanting her out of the way. Now the time when you went to her apartment, was there no other reason why you wanted to see her other than what you'd heard about your losing the picture?"

"No, that was my reason for going."

"You're quite sure that it wasn't something to do with a photograph?"

I shot the last word at him and got results. He started and threw a questioning glance at Naomi.

"I've told him about it, Dad," she said in a low, halting voice.

His shoulders sagged, he seemed to age ten years. He turned a haggard face to me.

"The photograph was another reason for my going," he admitted.

"I see. Then that gives you an additional motive—to save your daughter's reputation and that of her baby."

He nodded listlessly.

"I would like to know where you obtained the curare that you used on the knife."

He took a long time to answer. Finally he said, "I got it from a friend."

"What friend?"

"I'll keep his name a secret. I admit only that I had some curare and that I used it on the knife."

"There is another thing that isn't quite clear. You say that you dropped the knife?"

"Yes."

"You're sure of that?"

"Yes, I'm sure of it."

"How did you know that we were questioning Naomi again? Who told you?"

I could see the corners of his mouth tighten.

"Another friend, perhaps," he said.

"St. Denis is a friend of yours, then?" I suggested.

He merely shrugged.

"When you came to the lounge here you saw that your daughter was breaking under the cross-examination and because you loved her dearly you decided to give yourself up rather than allow her to be tortured. Is that correct?"

"It is."

"Because you feared that she had killed Zara. She was trying to protect you." I leaned back in the settee and smiled at him. "You know, Frank—I think both you and Naomi are very grand people."

A look of consternation flashed across both their faces, then vanished to be relieved by a smile.

"You were trying to protect someone when I questioned you earlier. Naomi refused to talk because she was worried. I didn't know that you were related but I sort of classed you together. I had to make you talk, had to trap you. I did. It worked beautifully—you came charging to her rescue. I'll say again that I think you're both very grand and nice people, and that in spite of a very convincing story, you had nothing to do with the murder. You're a good liar, Frank, your dialogue is good, you have a swell imagination but you did not have all the facts. The knife was not dropped. It was plunged into the sand at the bottom—purposely. There is just one thing I'd like to know—how did you find out that curare was used to kill Zara?"

The sardonic smile on his face gave way to a boyish grin. "I'm afraid I was outside the window when you were cross-questioning the Rajah."

I grinned back, glad to know who it was.

"All right, Frank, you win. Run along now and see if you can both keep out of this mess and give me a chance to get some place. Oh, by the way, you needn't worry about anyone remembering anything about your secrets, either of you, eh, Rocky?"

The big fellow spoke fervently. "Hope to choke if I'd ever say anything to hurt Miss Ravelle or you, sir."

Frank was too overcome with emotion to say anything then; he just shook hands with me and my bloodhound. Naomi threw her arms around my neck and kissed me. She did the same to Vicky. Then she looked up at Rocky.

He was grinning.

"Do you mind if I kiss you too?" she asked.

His grin widened to a slit, he was brick-red but he managed to say, "I—I'd love it, Miss Ravelle."

She gave him three generous osculations; then, arm in arm with her father, she turned to leave.

Halfway to the door Frank stopped and swung about.

"Dean, old man, there's one thing I'd like to know."

"Shoot," I said.

"Who did kill her, since you're so sure I didn't?"

"I've no idea and if I knew I wouldn't jeopardize your safety by telling you. Goodnight."

He gave me a deep bow, then cleared out with his beautiful daughter.

Vicky gave me a good big kiss and told me that I was a darling. I agreed with her. Rocky was staring after Naomi and Frank.

"Oh, Rocky," I said, but there was no reply. That kiss of Naomi's had definitely done things to him. I tried again. "OH, ROCKY!"

That brought him out of the ether or wherever he was. He spun quickly on his heel.

"Get me Basil St. Denis—if he's not in his cabin, you might try Miss Ravelle's." That one went under his hide, but he lumbered off.

"Might as well finish the job," I said to Vicky.

CHAPTER FIFTEEN

VICKY WAS MAKING a business of thinking. Elbow on table and little chin cupped in one hand—she was staring glassily at the table-top. The remarkable thing about her was that she always looked as if she'd just stepped out of a bandbox. Here it was about four in the morning and her skin had that cool, opalescent glow, and what little make-up she used still looked fresh and intriguing. Most females around this hour would have mascara and lipstick smeared all over the shop.

I said, "Vicky, you're the most beautiful thing I've ever seen."

There was a cute little creamy gap where her sweater had crept away from her slacks. I slid one arm around her waist. She laid her head on my shoulder and said, "I know I am."

I lost track of my hand for a moment.

She took my hand, slapped it and gave it back to me.

"Mr. Mallory,"—there was a mischievous light in her eye—"remember you're not a senator—one investigation at a time, if you please."

I gave a little bow.

"Your pardon, miss—I didn't realize what I was doing."

"How unoriginal, Mr. Mallory—that's the excuse we girls have used for years—and years!"

I was in the middle of rumpling her hair, when Rocky returned with St. Denis. The latter was looking very pleased with himself.

"Well, Mallory, what can I do for you this time?"

Ignoring his flippant mood, I gave him one of my celebrated frozen-faced stares and said, "Nothing—nothing at all for me. This has nothing to do with the investigation, St. Denis, but if I were in your shoes and had behaved as rottenly as you have toward a lovely little girl whom we both know—I'd do my best to make up to her for all the misery I'd caused her."

He started to get angry—then changed his mind and grinned.

"Thanks, old man—that's a swell idea. I've already taken care of that; we've talked it over."

As he got to his feet my bloodhound horned in. His lower jaw protruded ominously. "And if you don't marry her—I'm going to break your beautiful neck."

St. Denis gave him a tricky salute.

"Okay, big boy—if I don't you've got my permission."

With that he oiled out.

Rocky stroked his rock-ribbed chin thoughtfully, muttering aloud, "Maybe I'm wrong—maybe that guy ain't a pansy after all."

I turned to Vicky.

"Listen, precious," I said, "I've a confession to make."

"Well?" came her guarded reply. "Don't tell me you killed her."

"No, I find myself in need of a drink."

She wrinkled her little nose at me. She pursed her lips and gave me an appraising look.

"Oh—so that's the kind of a peanut-vender you are, no moral fiber. You swear off drinking to impress me, and an hour later you want to jump off the wagon. I can see that my marital bliss is just going to be one long session of cork pulling."

I slid an arm around her—her shoulders this time.

"I love your eyes—the way they turn up at the ends slays me; I love your lips; I love the way you do your hair; I love your . . . well ... I love everything about you, and I hope that from the moment our honeymoon begins, tea, coffee and milk'll be my only liquid vices. But now, I want to solve this ghastly mess and I'm feeling blotto. Therefore, no drinks—no solution, because I'm dead on my feet."

Vicky stopped wrinkling her nose.

"All right—you old soak," she laughed, "but remember—after we're married—let me hear so much as a single burp and it'll be just too bad for you."

I banged the brow thrice on the table by way of acknowledging the concession, and said, "Fine—swell! Now, I tell you what we'll do. Fanny tells me that if I sit on this gawd-awful settee much longer I'll have to spend my honeymoon eating off the mantelpiece. This place is beginning to give me the heebies anyway. We'll go to your cabin. You can lie down and get your beauty sleep; then, if Rocky will dig up some highballs, I'll bend the brain and see what can be done about solving this hodge-podge."

"What d'you want, Scotch or Rye?" Rocky asked with an eagerness that suggested a great thirst.

I ordered Scotch.

"Bring me one too," Vicky cried.

Rocky grinned approval and headed for the bar.

"Think you have the answer?" she asked.

"As the district attorney would say, 'The case rests,'" I replied.

"Let me hear your brain work," she said impishly.

We went on deck because Rocky was to meet us at Vicky's cabin with the drinks. The fog was still very thick, worse than it had been the last time we went out for air.

A radio was going full blast in one of the cabins. The light was on, the window open. I was right—it was Betty Potter. She was sitting up in bed playing solitaire. She seemed to be completely defrosted—unfortunately. Nobody else would have such a total disregard for other people. If she wanted to play the radio, she'd play it—no matter if the rest of the world slept or not.

We reached Vicky's cabin, opened the door and switched on the lights. On the floor beside Vicky's torn white harem dress lay a pile of feminine garments; on the bed reposed a beautiful girl. The lady was lying flat on her back with an arm thrown across her face. She seemed to be asleep. I recognized her immediately by the footprints on her stomach. It was the girl we'd galloped over in the saloon.

Vicky peeked over my shoulder and said.

"Oh!"

I asked, "A friend of yours? Does it belong here?"

"It most certainly does not," she said testily.

On hearing our voices, the lady opened one bleary eye.

"Don't mind me, folks—I'll move over."

"You most certainly will," exclaimed Vicky—with no little force, "over to another cabin." The girl sat up and yawned, then shrugged her shoulders.

"Okay! If you feel that way about it. All I've got to say is, this is one hell of a party. First they murder somebody, then they walk all over you."

She slid off the bed and began gathering her clothes into a bundle.

"Here we are, Chief— *Holy Mackerel!*"

Rocky'd arrived with a trayful of highballs and nearly dropped it when he saw what the fog had blown in. I tried to reassure him.

"It's all right, Rocky—the little lady got in the wrong cabin by mistake. Perhaps you'll be good enough to help her find an empty one?"

Rocky parked the highballs on a table and gave me a pleading look. I turned to the girl.

"Pardon the suggestion, but don't you think you'd better put something on before you leave? It's foggy outside and sailors are broadminded, but ..." I paused for emphasis.

She realized her scant attire, yanked a quilt from the bed, draped it about her body and handed her bundle to a perspiring Rocky.

"Home, James!" she said, and led the way out into the fog.

Rocky gave me one forlorn look and clumped after her.

I lifted a couple of highballs off the tray and handed one to Vicky. We sat on the edge of the bed and sipped our drinks while attempting to regain our equilibrium.

After the bracer I began to feel better.

"You know," she said, "I'm sorry you undid that rope, especially since there are beautiful, practically nude females leaping about the decks."

I could see her point.

"Then you don't trust me?" I said—a trifle piqued, be it known.

She smiled sweetly at me.

"Don't be absurd! Of course, I do—at the end of a rope and not a very long one either. And while we're on the subject—" She paused for a moment. "I'm going to ignore that crack St. Denis made about you and Zara. But don't try any new angles in the future."

Rocky came back sporting the beginning of a black eye. I squinted at him over the rim of my highball.

"Rocky—I'm surprised at you," I teased. "I thought you were a nice home-loving soul. Did you run into an open door?"

The corners of his mouth dropped—he was embarrassed.

"It wasn't my fault. I accidentally stepped on the end of that quilt she was wearing, and it came off. She turns, and says, 'You big white slaver!' hauls off and socks me in the eye. Believe me, that dame packs a mean wallop."

I could hear Vicky chuckling behind me.

"Did you find her a cabin?" I inquired.

"I did not!" was the indignant reply. "I just said, 'Nerts to you, sister,' threw her clothes at her and cleared out.

He went into the bathroom. I heard water running.

Presently he returned holding a wet towel to his bad eye. He pulled up a chair and sat down at the table.

"What do we do now?" he asked.

I picked up a pencil and pushed a sheet of paper in front of me.

"Now," I said, "I'd like to estimate just what we have at the moment. I'm going to tell you what conclusions I've arrived at so far, so that, in case we do solve the murder, you'll be able to give a good, plausible yarn to the papers."

The untoweled half of his face gave me a grateful look.

"That's sure swell of you," he said.

"I know it is. I'm really an awfully nice fellow, my friends tell me I am—when they use the touch system. But remember this—if we don't solve this case you still get all the credit." His grateful grin grew broader than ever.

"We'll start off with Sid Tricker. He was in a spot— married to the girl, his own divorce not yet final in this country, and she had him tied up with a long-term picture contract. Sid expected to make a lot of money out of her, and was probably willing to be blind to her blatant cheating. I say probably. In his own way, he loved her, and no doubt was egotistical enough to feel that he'd get her back again sooner or later. On the other hand, he may have realized that she'd never be his. He planned the trip, knew every move before it was made, had much to gain from her death. If he didn't kill her he must have a sense of relief. If he did, he hopes to keep out of the clutches of the law.

"Next, we have this chap Julma Desa—the Rajah. He's indirectly mixed up in it. I feel sure that the curare Zamper obtained for Michael Sarakov came from this fellow's father in Ciudad Bolivar on the Orinoco. There are some more questions I'd like to ask him. He's still a Number One possibility.

"Basil St. Denis is just a very conceited, spoiled young man with underlying good qualities which I hope will come to the surface as a result of all this, but he is neither intense nor definite enough in his emotions to commit a murder. He also must be relieved to know Zara is dead. It's not likely but it's remotely possible that he killed her.

"Frank Lane, on the other hand, is a man capable of great love, also of great hatred—an inheritance, no doubt, from his Spanish mother. So far, he has the best motives for wishing Zara out of the way. The opportunity that he'd worked for years to get, he was about to lose through her, also the good name and future happiness of the one thing he loved—his daughter—were at this woman's mercy. As you know, the story he told of how he committed the murder was full of holes. I think he was actually afraid that Naomi had killed Zara. Like her father, Naomi was capable of extremes in emotion. She would ħave liked to kill Zara. She admitted that, but she has a long head and had considered every angle. Also, there was her baby—if the murder were pinned on her there would be no chance of his ever getting a name. So I put them off the suspect list."

Rocky noticed that my highball had reached an all-time low, and thoughtfully handed me another from the tray. I thanked him, snipped two inches off the top, and carried on.

"This narrows the field somewhat, takes us back to Zamper and Sarakov."

"Zamper, we know, lived chiefly by his wits. Entered this country illegally about two years ago, and has been making a living by chiseling around with Oriental rugs among the movie crowd. He's been doing quite well by blackmailing Zara because of what he knew about her past. It is therefore reasonable to suppose that he also made it his business to know the source from which she was getting the money. I feel pretty certain that he knew Grey had the ten thousand with him and that, after Zara had been killed, he went into Grey's cabin, probably while I was questioning him, and took the money. So far, I can't see what he had to gain by her death. True—he was about to be deported, but she had promised him the ten thousand, so—why would he want to kill her? Even after having been deported, he could probably have continued drawing dividends on the knowledge he possessed of her past. No—I can't see Zamper going for murder—he hasn't got the guts, for one thing, and he's not the type to kill the goose that lays the golden eggs. And yet if she felt strong enough to defy him, if she burned the plans in front of him, if she knew he was to be deported, she may have been willing to risk his anger. Under such events he might have planned to kill her.

"That leaves us with Michael Sarakov. The man's something of an enigma. When I was questioning him, he admitted meeting Zara in a night club about a year ago. Now, thanks to Henry Grey, we know that Sarakov brought her to this country from the Orient. We've also learned that he was a close enough friend of the manager of the club to get him to feature her in his floor show with the sole purpose of having her meet Henry Grey. Again, according to Grey's information, the Secret Service is watching this manager—suspecting him of being a foreign agent. Off-hand, I'd say that he and Sarakov are working for the same government with the particular object at the moment of obtaining all the data on Grey's airplane motor. They probably looked pretty thoroughly into Grey's private life and discovered that he was inclined to be a woman chaser. It's a Hitlerian tactic, we know. They laid their plans well—they got hold of Zara, taught her enough about planes for her to be able to talk intelligently on the subject—and landed Mr. Grey."

"Then that makes Sarakov a spy," Vicky said.

I agreed. "And there was just one thing he over-looked—Zara was an opportunist. Sid Tricker had met her at the night club before she met Grey. He must have, because as soon as she had got hold of the plans she high-tailed it for Los Angeles. Sid had probably been interested in her and had told her to come and see him if she came to Hollywood. Being a smart girl she decided that she'd be foolish to turn the plans over to Sarakov, when Grey could be counted on to come through handsomely—later she could make a deal with the big Russian. The Russian was either so madly infatuated with her that—so long as he could be near her—although he knew she was holding out on him, he was content to let things ride, or else she stalled him off with some cock-and-bull story—probably the latter.

"Now if, as Grey claims to be the case, she was really intending to return the plans in exchange for another ten thousand, that would mean that she was definitely giving Sarakov the double-cross. I think that somehow or other he found out about her plans ahead of time, laid his own plans and, at the right moment—murdered her. Working on the theory that everyone of us has a screw loose some place, his loose screw was in thinking that by killing her that way he would not be suspected. We know that Sarakov had some curare in his possession. Zamper tipped him off about this diving stunt in advance. Why, I don't know. He had the opportunity to commit the murder, and knew Zara had the plans of the plane motor with her. The plans we found burned. The only thing that makes me at all doubtful that Sarakov's our man, is the apparent genuine grief he showed when he brought her body into the lounge—he's either a damned fine actor or else he really loved the girl, maybe both."

"Your mind is made up about Zamper, isn't it?" Rocky asked.

"I'm just thinking out loud. The only people I'm willing to dismiss are Frank Lane, Naomi and Betty Potter. Zamper is the best suspect so far."

"What about Grey?" Vicky asked.

"He doesn't seem quite the type but one never knows," I answered.

I leaned back and buried my nose in the highball. A pair of warm arms slid around my neck. She rested her head on my shoulder and beamed at Rocky.

"Isn't he wonderful? He's told us everything but who killed her. Sometimes I think he's almost intelligent."

"It isn't so easy," Rocky said, coming to my defense. "There's a motive for all of them and they were all in the water. What we need is something definite and conclusive."

"I wish there was some way of getting to the bottom of it right here," Vicky said. "I don't like the idea of waiting."

"It won't be long now," I promised her with more

assurance than I felt.

"Want me to put Zamper in the clink?" Rocky asked hopefully.

I shook my head. Rocky thought I meant an answer to his question when in reality I was realizing that I had downed two highballs in rapid succession. That, they tell me, is how drunkards are made. I was tired, the drinks had bucked me up, there was still a lot to be done and, well, there was Vicky, looking rather tired and drawn herself. I thought of coffee and suggested another go at it.

They were willing enough and we were all set to go when Sarakov loomed in the door.

CHAPTER SIXTEEN

SARAKOV WAS A majestic creature. There was a relentlessness about him as he marched in, a grim determination, a sense of invincibility. Even then, carrying a bath towel caught and held by the corners, he was a regal figure. Secretly I admired the man and yet I still had some doubt about him. To believe him guilty was one thing, to prove his guilt would be quite another. That bath towel intrigued me and when it was opened my suspicions of him vanished.

"This will be of interest to you," he said and dropped the towel on the table.

We moved forward. Rocky's face fell. Vicky said, "Oh." I was stumped by what I saw. The bath towel contained a bath sponge, no more and no less.

"Do you want to find a bathtub?" I asked.

"No, my friend. There is a bath connected with my cabin. An attempt has been made on my life, with that," he pointed a finger at the sponge.

I stepped forward and would have picked it up but he brushed me aside with a sweep of his great arm. "You think I jest," he said. "Look!"

He lifted two empty highball glasses and pressed them down on the sponge. A large spiked hook came up out of the sponge. My hand went forward. "Do not touch it," he warned. "It is full of hooks."

"What the hell?" Rocky gasped.

"I suppose they are mine too," Vicky cried.

"Probably," Sarakov agreed. He released the glasses. The sponge sprang back into shape, the hooks vanished.

"Tell me about it," I said.

"That sponge I bought in San Pedro before coming aboard the yacht. A few minutes ago I decided to bathe. The sponge was in a paper bag just as it had been given to me in the drugstore, or so I thought. I shook it from the bag into the tub. It made a rasping sound as it struck. Fortunately I heard that slight sound. I shudder to think what my fate would have been if I had filled the tub as I so often do before throwing in the sponge. As it was I thought that perhaps there had remained on the sponge some slight piece of shell. There often is on a cheap sponge, you know, and this was not expensive. As I bent over the tub I noticed a yellow deposit on the enamel. My curiosity was aroused immediately. It was curarine. Look!" With a finger he gingerly rolled the sponge over and in the towel under it there was the yellowish powder he mentioned.

Rocky asked, "What would have happened to you?"

"I would have died as Zara died—horribly." He shuddered; so did I, for that matter. "If I had punctured myself with any one of those hooks the curarine would have finished me."

"What a horrible way to kill a person!" Vicky cried.

"But I did not die, my dear," he said.

"You sure were lucky," Rocky agreed.

"But there will be more attempts," he said bitterly. "Other efforts."

"Who wants to get rid of you?" I asked.

"Ah, if I only knew, then we would have the person who killed her."

"But you must know something about the murder, have some information dangerous to the murderer. What is it?" I insisted.

"If I but knew, Mallory. I have racked my brain trying to think back. If I have information it escapes me at the moment."

"Since your life is in danger we must do something to protect you. You really need a bodyguard," I said.

"No. I have been warned. I've been saved by a miracle. I am on guard now, I will not die, not that way. I do not need a bodyguard. I will go back to my cabin, lock myself in and wait for the dawn and the police." He turned and started across the cabin.

"Go with him, Rocky, to his cabin, see that he is safe," I suggested.

"Thank you, Mallory, I do not need your man."

"Go with him anyhow," I insisted.

They left together.

"What are we going to do with that?" Vicky asked.

"We'll have to keep it. It's evidence, dangerous evidence to have around. We'll have to find some safe place to hide it, to keep it away from people and Shang."

I made a tour of the room and finally located a locker which seemed to be the safest place I could find at the moment. I had just dropped it, towel and all into place and had closed the locker lid when a wild cry for help rang out.

I turned and dashed across the room to the door.

"Careful!" Vicky warned, coming up behind me. "It may be a trap."

I heard footsteps running along the deck and then the cry again. Rocky barged up to the door. "I thought it was you!" he said, relieved.

Cabin doors popped open, heads came out and the cry continued.

"It's the Rajah!" someone said. "Must be having a nightmare!"

It was Desa, the Rajah, but he was not having a nightmare, not the regular kind. He stood away from his window and continued to cry for help with hysterical repetition.

"Let me in!" I shouted. "What is the trouble?"

He stopped. I saw him move toward the door. I heard the bolt click, the door opened. Shang darted in. Desa howled. Rocky and Vicky followed. As I looked back a wall of faces seemed to fill the door. Lane, Grey, St. Denis, Zamper and many curious people. Sid was there too, asking questions, demanding answers.

I went back and asked them to return to their cabins. "But what goes on?" Sid demanded. "I ought to be allowed to know."

I could see Betty, a little late for this event, straining on tiptoe to see into the cabin.

"I'll see you in the bar, later," I promised Sid and closed the door, went to the window and pulled down the blind.

Desa stood in the center of the room holding a red morocco slipper in his hand. Shang sniffed about his legs. Vicky and Rocky were looking from Desa's face to the slipper, wondering what had caused the outcry.

"Well, Desa?" I said.

The man's calm was returning slowly. I was willing to give him a little time to gain control of himself. His cabin was on the starboard side of the yacht. I heard the murmur of voices die away outside and then Betty's radio polluting the air like Sadie Thompson's talking machine.

"I have been very childish," he finally said. "Now, I am ashamed. I saw the face of death and it terrified me."

"When? How?" I asked.

"Here." He extended the slipper toward me. "I was getting ready to take a nap. It has been a long night. My friend Zamper gave me these slippers. I intended to wear them. I sat down to take off my shoes when I remembered a small box of curare in my possession. I was afraid to keep that box and was suddenly filled with the thought that it must be concealed. I did not know what to do with it. For a moment I considered throwing it overboard but I knew that would be useless. The water is clear here, it would be seen on the bottom. I could not let it remain in the open; there will be a search when the police arrive. I took the box and jammed it into this slipper. It would not go in."

He looked at us, his big eyes wider than ever before. "I was puzzled, tried to ram the box in again but it would not go. When I drew it out I saw some curare on its end. That puzzled me. I had not used the curare. I took a knife and cut the top of the slipper. Look!"

Our three heads were together as he opened the two

pieces of the slipper. No wonder the little box would not go in when he pushed it. Imbedded in the sole of the shoe a razor blade's edge, smeared with curare, stood up.

"Ugh!" Vicky mumbled and turned away sickened by the possibilities of that sharp edge. She had realized that a foot thrust into the slipper would have been parted by that thin blade.

"No wonder you had the jitters," Rocky said. "What a mind this murderer must have!"

"Ingenious," I admitted. I took the slipper from Desa. "This must be put in a safe place."

"We ought to take that blade out," Rocky suggested.

"Not until we have a pair of pincers. It's too dangerous to risk even a slight nick," I said.

"Your plan seems to be working," Vicky said.

"Too well," I admitted and shivered. "Two people have narrowly escaped death."

"Three," she reminded me.

"Three?" Desa repeated.

"A knife was thrown at me. An attempt has just been made on Sarakov and now you," I explained.

Desa gave a great sigh.

"What do you know about Zara's death?" I asked.

"Nothing."

"Then why this attempt on your life?"

"The curare probably," he replied slowly. "My father sends it to me. I sell it to Zamper. This box just came today before I left for the yacht."

"Why did you bring it with you?"

"Zamper told me he needed some more. I supposed it was for Sarakov. I thought it would make it easy for Zamper to deliver it directly."

I took the box, looked at my fingers to be sure there were no cuts of any kind, and opened the lid. When I had seen the box earlier in the night its surface had been smooth, untouched. Now it showed clearly that some of its contents had been taken out.

I looked at Desa. "Who used this?"

He pointed at the slipper.

"Who knew you had this extra supply?"

"Zamper, but he told me he would not need it. After the murder I told him I wanted to get rid of it. He told me to wait, that he would find a way."

"Looks like we been skinning the bark off the wrong tree," Rocky said.

"Put this slipper away," I ordered. "There is no need to warn you to be careful for the rest of the night. Lock yourself in."

"Must I stay here alone?" he cried.

"You're as safe here as anywhere. We can't watch you and there are not enough men to detail as bodyguards," I explained as we prepared to leave.

We stood just outside his door, heard the lock click behind us.

"The fog's still dirty," Rocky said, "but it'll be daylight in about an hour. It's been quite a night."

"And quite a case. Everything's dirty tonight."

"Yeah," Rocky agreed.

"Let's go to Zamper's cabin."

Our progress was halted by Shang. His hangover made him temperamental. He growled and complained for perhaps two or three minutes before he was willing for us to start. When we did get going he yipped and got in the way. The little devil wanted to be carried. I can't stand nagging so I finally bent down and tucked him under my arm.

Rocky stopped before a door. "This is it," he said. The cabin was dark. Rocky reached a hand inside to grope for the light.

"Don't do it that way, Rocky," I warned.

"Why not?"

"Since our murderer is being so ingenious a pin stuck in the light switch would be a swell way to kill any one of us."

His arm came out rapidly.

"I'll press the button with a key," he said. I could hear

him scratch about with a piece of metal until the light went on. "I don't like this Zamper fellow," he said.

The cabin was empty.

"Nor do I," I agreed. "I have a confession to make to you both. I've been awful dumb. Zamper is the man who killed Zara."

"But I thought you said you weren't sure," Vicky protested.

"I wasn't then. Zamper told me he couldn't write and I didn't believe him at the time. He can write. He wrote that note that Shang found under her bed. He'd been blackmailing Zara. She was to have given him money tonight and didn't. He was afraid of her. Through his friend Desa he knew about the plans for this party. He planned it, all right."

"Why didn't you tell me to arrest him?" Rocky asked.

"He can't get away."

"Maybe he can't but he isn't in here," Vicky stated baldly.

We were standing in the door when we heard it.

"What was that?" Vicky whispered and clutched at my arm.

Before either Rocky or I could reply there was a splash which seemed to come from up toward the bow.

"Probably a gull diving for a fish," Rocky suggested

"Then they must be wearing fog lights," Vicky said.

"Vicky's right—the fog's too thick—I thought I heard a muffled human cry."

"Sea-gulls," he insisted.

"Man overboard!" sounded ahead of us.

A form loomed ahead in the fog. Rocky reached out and gripped it. There was a short struggle, a couple of grunts and one startled, "What the hell!" and it was all over. Rocky had tangled with a deckhand.

He had, he said, heard a peculiar cry. He ran forward and had seen someone duck through the fog ahead, had heard the splash. He had sounded the warning and then Rocky had grabbed him.

The searchlight sprang to life on the bridge but it couldn't cut through the fog, just moved in a luminous circle against the white bank of the soggy night.

Cabin doors popped open.

"What happened—who went overboard?"

Rocky was leaning over the rail. "Whoever it was in this fog—we won't find him. He'll probably make the shore but he won't get away from the Island."

I, too, leaned over the rail. Rocky was right, in that blanket of mist there wasn't a ghost of a chance of finding the man.

The captain joined us. He listened to the deckhand, stroked his blue chin thoughtfully and said, "No use trying to pick him up. We'll notify the shore. Probably someone trying to make a getaway."

Rocky looked at me for instructions.

"Check the cabins and keep your eye out for Zampcr," I said.

We moved along the deck. The fog stuck to my hair, saturated my robe. Shang shook himself and complained, burrowed inside the robe. A door opened near us. It was Sarakov.

"Anything wrong?" he asked.

"I think Zamper has made a getaway," I replied.

"Zamper!" He ran a hand over his damp hair. "Why?"

"Too much has happened, too many things point directly to him. He's trying to escape," I said.

CHAPTER SEVENTEEN

WE WENT BACK TO Zamper's cabin, which was a disappointment. There wasn't a great deal there. A shaving outfit, a pair of gaudy silk pajamas, and a blue brocaded robe with his initials on the breast pocket. The fellow had been going ritzy, all right. In a closet hung a natty, green tweed sport suit, a tan shirt, tie to match and a pair of brown oxfords. I went through the pockets of the suit. They yielded nothing of importance.

While I was going through the clothes, Vicky had been sitting thoughtfully on the edge of the bed. I'd just got through finding nothing when she spoke.

"Doesn't it seem strange that a man'd try to escape while wearing funny clothes—when he had a perfectly good tweed suit available? A man wandering around in an Arab's pants'd be bound to arouse suspicion."

"Good for you, Vicky—that's just what I've been thinking."

"Well, why didn't he change his clothes?" she demanded.

"He probably didn't want to take the time. He was smart, in his way."

"So that's the end of the murder," she said.

"That's the end. Come along. I'm going to put you to bed and then I'm going back to the *Parrakeet* to finish what is left of the night. When do we get married?"

"Some nice day next week," she said and kissed me.

As we went along the deck she said, "We haven't had our coffee, and, Dean, I'm cold."

"A word from Desa first," I said and started for his cabin.

I rapped twice before he answered guardedly.

"Open up, it's Mallory," I ordered.

He peered out at us. "What was the commotion?" he

asked.

"Zamper has left the boat."

"Oh," he said.

"We think he is trying to make a getaway. He knew all about the plans for this party, didn't he?"

Desa nodded.

"Did he know about the diving contest?"

"Yes. Perhaps that is it," he said slowly.

"What do you mean?"

"On the way over, Zamper, Sarakov and I were having a drink in here. We were discussing the party, laughing about the whole idea. I showed them the pink pearls and the bag filled with the red stones. I remember tying the bag securely and putting it on the dresser. When I returned for the bag tonight, it had been opened. I'm sure some of the stones had been taken."

"Is that so!" I snorted. "You told me you knew nothing about the rubies until Tricker gave you the bag just before the stunt."

"I was afraid, afraid of Zamper and Sarakov. I was in the position of the man who knows too much. My slipper proves I was right."

"That's it," I said. "Zamper took some of those stones so that he would have an alibi of sorts after the murder. A man who had red stones to show could not have had time to knife her. Zamper wanted you out of the way so that you could not give this story to the police. Now all we'll have to do is wait for the police and daylight."

We left him and went to the galley. Between them, Rocky and Vicky made some very good coffee. We were there a half-hour or longer. It was getting gray outside.

"Well, the night's over," Rocky said with relief. "Thanks to you, Mr. Mallory, we know who did it, even if he did get away."

"Did you send word ashore?" I asked. I had forgotten all about that.

He nodded. "The captain sent a man in. They'll notify the mainland, and all vessels, to keep an eye out for him.

I don't believe he'll try to get away until the fog lifts."

The door opened behind us and the deckhand came in. "I got your man," he said. "Bumped into him on my way back from shore. Deader than a smelt and all puffy. Thought you'd like to know. He's up on deck." He had been at the sink as he talked, washing his hands. He went to the stove and filled a tin mug with coffee. "It's cold on the water," he said.

My whole case had gone to hell with those few callous words. Zamper dead! Puffy! Then he had been murdered. His was the choked human cry I had heard.

Vicky giggled. It was a form of hysteria.

"It's a hell of a mystery," I said, getting up. "I was sure Zamper had killed Zara and it wasn't just the fact that he tried to get away either."

"The murderer killed him," Vicky said.

My answer was one word, "Nuts!"

I was mad, sore as a boil, but there was no point in trying to explain to them something I couldn't explain to myself. There were things for me to do.

They followed me out of the galley to the deck.

"What do we do now?" Rocky asked helplessly.

"We'll take a look at Zamper," I said. "And then I'm going to have a drink."

The deckhand's description had been perfect. Zamper had died as Zara had died—curare. There was a wound on his neck, a short gash. I turned and went to the bar, thoroughly mad.

I fixed a stiff drink, one for each of us and sat down.

"What do you make of it?" Rocky asked.

"It doesn't make sense. You couldn't write a thing as screwy as this. Nobody would believe you. I was so sure Zamper killed her. He was next to her when they dove overboard. He knew the rubies were fakes, had some which he stole for an alibi. He said he dove in for the fun of it. He told me he couldn't write but he did write on the pad when Betty was trying to frame us. When I mentioned the slave market at Teheran he fell for that. It was a dead give-away."

"And now we'll have to start all over again," Vicky said.

She came over and sat on my lap and gave me an odd look. Large tears welled into her eyes—her lower lip trembled. "I'm sorry, Dean, awfully sorry."

"We'll get to the bottom of it," I promised.

Sid came into the bar and fixed himself a drink. "It's getting worse," he said. "The publicity I mean. One murder is bad enough, but two . . ." He shook his head dolefully.

"This second one is going to be easy," I promised.

"Easy, Dean?" he asked tonelessly.

I found myself feeling sorry for him again. He really was a good scout. His grand plan for publicity had turned into such a mess. It might ruin him. He knew it, too, as he stood there facing us, his drink in his hand. As he gazed into the amber depths of his glass I knew he was seeing the possibility of his failure.

He looked at me. "Dean, I didn't kill her, honest to God I didn't. I loved her. I know she played me for a sucker but I didn't care. I was willing. She was nice to me, sometimes, I was glad of that."

Vicky was weeping again, not for Zara but for Sid standing there shamelessly admitting that a few crumbs of affection had been enough for him.

"Look, Sid," I said. "I don't want to be tough, and I don't want to spoil your publicity, but then you can't spoil a bad egg, can you?"

"Don't kid me no more, Dean. I can't take it."

I put an arm about him. "I'm not kidding. I mean that things are bad enough as they are, but the publicity will be terrific. If we can solve this thing by ourselves it will help, but it's an awful mess. There have been three failures and one successful attempt at murder since Zara was killed. There's a lot involved in this, perhaps your life and mine. If the fog lifts, the police, the coast guard, and reporters will be down on our heads. We have very little

time. I'm going to do what I can. I have three possible
suspects, three people who, according to my reasoning,
may be the murderer."

"Who are they?" he asked.

"Don't mention any names, Dean," Vicky warned. "It's
too dangerous. This second murder proves that the
menace is still aboard—lends a sinister touch to the
situation."

She was looking very pale and quite worried. It had
been a tough night for her but she was still game.

"What are you going to do?" Sid asked.

"Try another angle. I think I'll have another chat with
Sarakov. You needn't come this time," I said to Rocky.
"Rest yourself."

Our spirits somewhat restored by the drink, Vicky
and I went out on deck. "Who are your three suspects
now?" she asked in a whisper.

I spoke into the thin shell of her ear. "Sid, Desa and
Sarakov."

"What makes you think that?"

"The attempts on Desa and Sarakov were either made
by Sid, or they were framed by the murderer to take
suspicion from himself. Don't forget those burned plans,
all the things at stake for all three of them."

"Be careful, Dean," she begged.

We were at Sarakov's cabin, the lights were on. I
knocked, heard him stirring about and then a demand to
know who we were.

At the sound of my voice the door opened immediately
and without question.

I think the last drink was beginning to have an effect
on Vicky. She refused the chair Sarakov so gallantly
offered and began puttering about the room with Shang
tucked under her arm. I sat down opposite Sarakov.

For a moment the man's eyes followed Vicky, then he
smiled and said, "She's a beautiful girl—Mr. Mallory. She
has a bewitching beauty that is very rare."

I lit a cigarette.

"So everyone's been telling me."

He laughed, then shot me a questioning look.

"There was, perhaps, something you wished to ask me?"

I nodded. "Yes, there are one or two things I would like to have cleared up. Er—you told me, I believe, that you met Zara in a night club in San Francisco about a year ago—didn't you?"

"Yes—I told you that. Actually I got her that job, didn't I tell you? I brought her over from Shanghai."

"But you pretended to know nothing about her and her past, is that true?"

"Yes."

"Why?"

"I didn't want our friendship to be misconstrued. The tongues of Hollywood are not kind to a girl under such circumstances."

I was fencing words with an expert—it was going to be very difficult to pin him down to anything tangible. I shifted my attack.

"This Russian who managed the night club, what was his name—?"

"Ivan Krassin."

"Thank you—yes, that was it. Was he a particular friend of yours?"

"He was my cousin," was the reply.

"I see. And you used this relationship to get him to feature Zara in his floor show?"

"We had also been brother officers in Von Ungern's White Army operating against the Bolsheviks in Siberia —there is little that we would not do for one another."

I was going to ask if his sole purpose in getting her the job was not to contact Grey, but decided to save it for a later date. It would only serve to put him more on his guard, so I changed the subject.

"Now, about yourself, Mr. Sarakov," I continued, "you're pretty much the man of mystery in this part of the world. Of course you don't have to answer my question unless you want to, but I'm frankly curious to know from what sources you derive your income?"

He smiled pleasantly.

"You mean that most White Russians out here are penniless, having lost everything in the revolution, or are using that as the alibi for their poverty, while I, with no visible means of support, live in apparent luxury?" I nodded. "I have nothing to hide, Mr. Mallory. My father, who was killed in the revolution, was a noble, and a very wealthy man. Unlike the majority of the Russian nobility, he did not turn a deaf ear to the mutterings of the rabble; he sensed what was coming some years before the break actually came, and invested a considerable fortune in America. While nothing was salvaged from our estates in Russia, on my father's death, I inherited a considerable income from his holdings in this country."

It made a good plausible story, and I let him think that I was quite satisfied with it.

"You were indeed fortunate, Mr. Sarakov, to have such a wise father." He bowed his head slightly. "Now— what of Zara? We are both men of the world. You are a very forceful personality—not one to harbor a love in your heart for a girl without demanding more than to be allowed to be near her. I can far more easily picture you throwing her over your shoulder and stalking off to some mountain lair."

A great sadness came into his eyes. Damn it—guilty or not guilty, there was something about the man that made me feel as if I were committing sacrilege by probing into his private life.

For some moments he stared thoughtfully at the rip of his cigarette, then leaned back in his chair and fastened his great staring eyes on me.

"You wish to know of my love for Zara? Well, I shall tell you," he began. "It was a strange love, one that had its birth thirty years ago. You smile? But I assure you that it is the truth. I was a young officer in the Svodny Polk Regiment, the Czar's private guard, stationed at

Petrograd—St. Petersburg it was called in those days. I fell in love with a girl—a dancer. Every night I would sit at a table in the cabaret where she was employed. Eventually we became lovers. A few months later she told me that there was going to be a little one. I was desperately in love with her. If it had not been for my family I would have married her. In those days—unlike the modern generation—children were guided by their parents' wishes in all things, even after they had reached the age of manhood. When I spoke to my father about it he was very angry. He told me that ours was one of the proudest families all the Russias, that no member of our families had ever married beneath them. He sternly forbade my seeing the girl again." He paused, when he continued his voice was low. "That was .the only thing for which I never forgave him. And yet I realize that I was also to blame. If I had my life to live over again I would have married her in spite of the whole world. Like a coward I sent her a note telling her that I would be unable to see her again. The next morning it was found clutched in her small hand—she had taken poison.

"From that day on my father and I seldom spoke to one another. A wall had grown up between us that was insurmountable. I never married.

"When I met Zara she reminded me of the girl I loved. She swept back the years when she danced, and my beloved lived once more. I did not take her body—I did not want it. She was using it as a means to win her way to fame. The other girl loved me—I was the first and only man in her life."

His cigarette had burned down low, slowly he snubbed it out on an ashtray and lit a fresh one. I felt sorry for the man, somehow I felt that he'd been telling the truth—the part about Zara reminding him of the dead girl, anyway. At the same time I was sure that there was a whole lot that he wasn't telling.

"Mr. Sarakov," I said, "if, as you say, Zara reminded you of the girl you loved many years ago, mightn't you have wished to kill her because of the hold she had over you—to break the spell?"

Fire flashed in his eyes, he clenched his great fists.

"No—a thousand times, no!" he thundered. "The memories she brought back were the only things that made life worth living for me. You think that I am a perfect specimen of humanity, strong, rugged and healthy. But you do not know that here in my throat is a cancer that is slowly but surely shortening my days. I chose to spend them in what happiness this wretched world affords—I chose to spend them near Zara."

His great body relaxed its tension. He closed his eyes. When he opened them again, the fire had gone —they were just as expressionless and uncommunicative as before.

"I understand, Mr. Sarakov—I am sorry to have had to pry into your private affairs, but in cases of this kind people's innermost feelings have to go by the board. There is just one more thing I want to ask you before I go. That is—what do you know about Julma Desa?"

"I know very little about the man. I have talked with him a few times. Zamper had told me that Desa was born some place on the Orinoco and was familiar with the manner in which the natives make use of curare for hunting purposes. I was interested, naturally, and obtained some useful information from him I believe that he and Zamper had some business dealings together— ones that might not always be able to stand close scrutiny. However, I think that whatever money was made out of them, Zamper took the lion's share—Desa always appeared poorly dressed."

"Mr. Sarakov—Zamper was murdered within the last hour."

I was watching his face closely. The man had marvelous control—his expression remained unchanged, only his eyelids seemed to tighten at the far corners.

"That is good—that is Karma." He spoke as though pronouncing a death sentence. "You are sure that he was murdered?"

"Quite sure—curare was used."

"Ah! Then it is indeed Karma."

I knew a little bit about theosophy—by the Karma business he meant retribution.

"Why do you say that?" I asked.

The man turned those great staring eyes on me again —they were beginning to give me the creeps.

"That is a question that I shall not answer—yet." His voice held a note of finality. There was nothing more I could learn from him at this sitting without forcing the issue by bringing up the subject of the plans. When I did that, I wanted my big bloodhound Rocky with me, for I expected fireworks, and cancer or no cancer this fellow could raise one hell of a lot of dust if he ever went berserk; and I had no intention of supplying the dust if I could help it.

I eased the body out of the chair and gathered in my trailer. She was pretty glassy-eyed by this time.

"Well, Mr. Sarakov," I said, "I think that covers about everything for the moment. I may drop in again later."

"Then, Mr. Mallory, I shall be expecting you." He bowed gravely to Vicky.

We were at the door when he spoke again. "If I knew who had killed her I'd tear him apart with my two hands. Do you know?" he demanded.

"Not yet," I replied and shoved Vicky outside.

CHAPTER EIGHTEEN

IT WAS COLD ON deck, wet and damp, but I knew that somewhere the sun was shining; perhaps at Palm Springs it was hot and warm. There was a golden sheen to the fog. In a little while the sun would burn its way through, the fog would vanish. I found myself wishing that my confusion would go with it. I was floundering in a fog of my own trying to rearrange the cock-eyed pieces of the puzzle. Our time was getting short. I heard shore noises as the Island awoke; out in the channel I could hear the deep-throated blasts of annoyed shipping. Boats to and from the Orient, coastwise traders, tankers heading for El Segundo, they were all out there groping through a mist. They had instruments to help them. I must depend on a hunch, pure instinct.

Betty Potter's radio was still chattering away—some egg in Mexico was trying to sell his fellow eggs on something or other.

Sid loomed upon us, a dejected figure in a bathrobe wearing a dead cigar butt in his face. I didn't want to see people, I didn't want to talk, I wanted to think. I was annoyed because he happened to be there. Because I was annoyed with myself I took a poke at him with my alleged wit.

"Well, well!" I said. "If it isn't old man publicity himself."

He gave me a sour look. "Listen, Dean—will you forget that stuff? I never want to hear the word again."

I patted him on the shoulder. "Why, Sid—I'm surprised at you. Don't you realize that if the murder breaks properly it will be the most colossal piece of publicity ever given to a picture in the history of the motion picture business?"

He actually believed me. The cigar butt cocked itself

at the old rakish angle. He beamed, coming up out of the dumps like an old fire horse prancing at the sound of the gong. Suddenly he was himself again and began prodding me in the navel with his fat forefinger.

"You break this case, Dean, and I'll buy every novel you ever write—that is, if they're any good."

Leave it to Sid to put in a safety clause, even in conversation. He stopped his prodding and began rubbing his hands together. He was off, thinking of his business, of ways to capitalize on the publicity.

I gave him an accusing look and said, "Bribery and corruption, eh? Nothing doing, Sid; you can't do that to a Mallory—not when he knows about your secret marriage." He winced at that. "I'll make this bargain with you—if I break this case before the authorities come aboard I want you to do two things. Naomi gets the lead in *Blue Lagoon* and Frank Lane directs it."

"Anything you say, Dean—it's okay with me. Who do you think is guilty?"

"Sid," I replied, "you're a good fellow so I'll let you in on the secret. I think you killed her."

"What?" he gasped. The cigar butt dropped to the deck.

"Sure! Think of the publicity angle—Producer Slays Leading Lady. It's Stupendous!"

Vicky smiled. "He's kidding, Sid," she said.

His smile was sour. "No fooling, Dean—who did it?"

"I don't know, Sid. I'm trying to figure it out. Run away, will you, and give me a chance."

He moved over to the rail and stood there looking down at the water.

"Were you serious about him, Dean?" Vicky asked.

"No."

"Then it's Desa or Sarakov," she said.

"That's the trouble. I'm not sure; it doesn't jell."

I headed for the cabin, trying to think of a way out.

Rocky was there waiting for us. "Any luck?" he asked.

"Yes and no."

"I haven't been much help to you," he said with regret.

"Sherlock Holmes himself would have been no help this time," I admitted. "It's not so elementary."

I sat down to think back over the sequence of events, to review each step, to consider all the angles.

Vicky came and sat beside me. She leaned against me. I felt her head sag over. We sat that way for a long time. Suddenly she jerked awake, turned and gave me a funny look and said, "Guess what I've got!"

I didn't feel like a guessing game, didn't feel like anything pleasant at the moment. "I know—a hangover," I said.

She jumped to her feet and moved away. She shook her head as she went. I knew she was sliding one hand down the inside of her sweater and was fishing around. If I thought about it at all I supposed she was trying to locate her handkerchief. For a moment I felt some remorse and was sorry if I had hurt her feelings. She swung to face me. There were no tears in her eyes; in fact, they danced. I noticed a large bulge in the middle of her chest, a lump that I knew had not been there when we'd staged our dressing-up party.

With a final heave she pulled forth a silver box and put it on the table.

"Where did you get it, precious?" I asked.

"Swiped it," she announced proudly. "Found it on Sarakov's dressing-table."

I was annoyed and said, "Listen—Kleptomania, will you cut it out? We're supposed to be solving murders, not going around swiping things."

"But, Dean. It is the box we found in Zara's room, the one with the ashes in it. If he swiped it from her room, wasn't it all right for me to take it from him? Not to steal," she added, "but because we ought to know why he took it."

I was on my feet and across to the table while she talked. It was the jewel box. I lifted it and opened the lid. It was empty.

"I'm going out to get some air," I said. "You two stay here."

"No, Dean. I'm going with you."

There was no point in an argument. I was so groggy that air seemed a prime necessity.

We passed Grey's cabin. He was standing in the door with a towel around his middle like Mahatma Gandhi. He stepped back when he saw Vicky.

"I beg your pardon," he said. "I didn't think there would be anyone about."

"It's quite all right, Mr. Grey," Vicky said quickly. "I'm going to be married soon."

Grey raised an eyebrow.

"It's blackmail," I said. "She has the goods on me and wants my strong manly body; nothing else will do, so I must make the sacrifice."

"Is that so?" she asked indignantly. "Don't you believe him, Mr. Grey—the big baboon has been proposing to me every day for the past six months and tonight he found himself compromised, exposed to Betty Potter, and he is begging me to make a decent man of him again." She ended with a rippling laugh.

We walked up and down for ten or fifteen minutes. I needed more than air to show me the end of the riddle.

Vicky yawned and said, "Are we going to play Felix the Cat all day too? I'm tired. When're we going to bed?"

I led her back to the cabin.

Rocky was stretched out on the bed sound asleep. The eye the human doormat had smacked was a sight to behold. I think "moldy plum" described it rather well.

I slammed the door shut and Rocky woke up. He was instantly contrite.

"I'm sorry. I just lay down for a minute and . . ."

"Quite all right," I told him. "How about going to the galley and seeing if you can rustle up some breakfast. I'm starved."

He grabbed his hat, jammed it on his head and cleared out, eager to atone for having been caught napping.

Vicky put Shang on the bed and curled up beside him. I plowed into the bathroom and doused my face in cold water—I felt better immediately. I dried my face on a towel, then plunked down on the bed beside Vicky.

She looked darned cute lying there asleep, her long black lashes glistening above a perfect complexion. I edged up close and kissed her. She slid an arm around my neck. Shang was jealous and protesting when the door opened and Rocky came in.

He had a trayful of ham and eggs, toast and coffee.

"How's that for service? The chef had this all ready for some of the gang in the saloon, so I just grabbed it in the name of the law."

The food smelled good. I wakened Vicky. Rocky planked the tray in the middle of the bed and perched himself on the side. We sat around Turkish fashion and fell to.

Shang chiseled in for a couple of eggs and a piece of toast—a reserve supply, as Rocky explained it, that he'd brought along just in case. Judging by the disappointed look in his eye I'll bet he could have killed Shang.

No word was spoken until we'd reached the cigarette stage; then, while Shang put the finishing touches to the platter I made my decision because the picture had at last taken form.

"Rocky," I said, "that piece of blue print that I found in the jewel box was part of the plan Zara stole from Henry Grey. Why she burned it—or why it was burned by someone else—I haven't the faintest idea, but I do know that Sarakov is mixed up in the deal and knows a hell of a lot more than he's already told. Now, we'll leave Vicky here and . . ."

"Oh no, you're not leaving me here," she objected. I was afraid of that.

"Listen, honey child! The fellow's in a spot. He's got a wild, insane look in his eyes and I think there'll be plenty of trouble when I call a showdown. I don't want you smeared all over the cabin."

"That's right," Rocky came nobly to back me up. "That guy's a bad baby—I don't trust them Russians —you'd better do as the Chief says."

Vicky began wrinkling her little nose at us, so I knew my scheme was sunk. She exhaled a cloud of smoke and then blew up—figuratively speaking, that is.

"I suppose you two lunatics think you can handle Sarakov beautifully—don't you? Well, I'm investing one perfectly good future husband in this deal, and I'm going along to take care of my investment."

And that was very much that. I carried on again.

"As I was saying, Rocky, the three of us, four with Shang, will shortly call on Mr. Sarakov and have a showdown. I want you to keep your eyes peeled for trouble and to have your gun handy, because I've a hunch that we're going to need it."

Rocky stuck out his chest.

"Leave it to me, Chief—the tougher they come the better I like it."

I was glad somebody was feeling optimistic.

"All right, boys and girls, here we go!"

I said it as cheerily as I could—inwardly it sounded to me like "famous last words."

We had to wait while Shang gave a few last licks to one of the plates, then Vicky tucked him under her arm and the expedition got underway.

Betty Potter's cabin was situated two doors from our destination—her radio was still going full blast; someone was giving a talk on care and maintenance of the human body. I was glad I didn't believe in omens. We knocked at Sarakov's door and his deep voice bade us enter.

CHAPTER NINETEEN

SAKAROV WAS SITTING at the far end of the cabin just as we had left him. He rose, bowed to Vicky, motioned us to be seated. He sank back into the chair in deep thought. A moody Russian, I decided. I had heard of that characteristic although I had never seen it in operation before. The Russians I have met have been gay, great eaters, good drinkers and a lot of fun. Don't get me wrong, I'm not talking about Russians who are Reds, but the other breed, the people who in their hearts have been saddened by the things happening in their great country.

"I was expecting you," he said gravely. He looked at Rocky, who had remained near the door leaning against the wall. "Sit down," he said. It was a command which even Rocky obeyed.

"There are a few more questions I want to ask you," I said.

"I've been expecting that too," he answered calmly.

"On our last visit here we, er—accidentally walked off with some of your property—this." I held the jewel box in front of me.

Damn the man—his control was superb, not a muscle of his face moved; he just sat there staring at me—waiting.

"It is yours—isn't it?" I asked.

"No, Mr. Mallory, it is not mine. It was Zara's. I gave it to her some months ago—it was a present. I knew you had taken it from me."

"Would you mind telling me how it came into your possession again?"

"I took it, why not?" he asked defiantly.

"Did you know what the box contained?"

His eyes darkened a trifle as he replied; a grim smile touched his lips. "Nothing but ashes."

"And do you know what those ashes were?"

"Yes, I know."

"So that is why you killed her," I said quietly. "Because she had burned the plans which she stole from Grey, the plans you wanted to sell abroad. I believed you when you told me you loved her, perhaps you did, yet your greed was so great that you killed her."

"No!" he boomed. "I did not kill her. You fool! Don't you know?"

His body went rigid—he kept his great staring eyes riveted on mine. I could sense Rocky stiffening behind me. Vicky was alarmed.

"I thought you were smart," he said insolently, "but you are stupid—like the others."

Betty's radio, which had been chattering away, suddenly blared forth loudly. She had evidently turned it up for some personal reason. It was at the end of a news broadcast and said:

"We have just learned that the murderer of Zara is one Jan Zamper. He escaped from the yacht during the night. All ships are warned to watch for him. Due to the fog which has separated the Island from the Mainland there is no further story in connection with the murder."

"The radio is smarter than you," Sarakov said.

The blaring voice died away again to a drone. Betty must have—well, never mind what she was doing for those few seconds.

"All right," I said. "I'm dumb, have been stupid all along, but I know who killed Zamper. This closes our case, Rocky," I said, turning round.

"No!" Sarakov boomed.

While I'd taken my eyes off him to speak to Rocky he had drawn a gun from his pocket. It was a snub-nosed automatic which he was pointing at my solar plexus. I froze instantly—never before had I realized how large the muzzle of an automatic could be. His eyes were blazing with an insane light. When he spoke, his lips scarcely moved. "If you try to arrest me, to handcuff me, I shall kill Mr. Mallory!"

I should have been prepared for just such an emergency and wasn't. Sarakov was right. I was as stupid as hell to face him that way.

I found myself longing for just two things—that my big bloodhound wouldn't try any heroics by going into action, and a crying need of some way out of our mess.

Rocky elected to stand pat, for which I was truly thankful. It was my trailer who went into action. She was the sanest person in the room. She didn't move—thanks be to Allah—she just spoke in a calm, low voice.

"Michael," she said, "do you mind if I ask you a question?"

Sarakov's face softened a trifle, but his eyes never flinched from mine, and his gun still pointed in my direction.

"Certainly, Miss Blaire," was the polite reply.

"Michael—do you want to ruin my future happiness?"

He was silent for a moment—then his low voice came again.

"How would I be ruining your future happiness?"

"Mr. Mallory is going to be my husband."

Followed another period of tense silence while he thought that over. Finally he spoke.

"Your husband, you say. Then I shall wed you in death and your friend will be the best man to help you across the Styx."

I saw Vicky's face blanch with horror. She bit her lips. I heard a sigh behind me. That was Rocky. I didn't dare look at him, didn't dare look anywhere but at that death-dealing muzzle. The man was mad, there could be no doubt of that. At any moment death, quick and certain, would spout from that little hole, such a little hole to do so much damage. I felt the beads of sweat standing out on my brow, knew one or two had trickled down into my eyebrows. I was trying to think but my brain was a blurr of little round holes which danced in front of my eyes. I felt rather than heard Rocky stir and I was terrified anew. One move would mean instant death.

I spoke but the words seemed to cleave to the roof of my mouth, sounded hollow and dry as they rattled out.

"Is it a lust for death, Sarakov? Do you enjoy killing? Weren't Zamper and Zara enough, or do you regret that your attempt on Desa failed?"

I saw his eyes flicker. "Desa?" he asked. Before I could control the muscles of my throat to speak again he went on. "You are doing this to distract me. So Desa escaped his destiny—Desa? That scum! He means nothing to me. You know so much. It is good that you die." The hand with the gun elevated a trifle.

"Now it's coming," I thought. "I hope he takes Vicky first. I don't want her to see . . ."

"I do this for my protection," he said. "Self-preservation. You've heard of that." His grin was horrible.

Vicky gulped. God, how I wanted to hold her in my arms to shut the sight of that gun away from her eyes! I wanted to live, to live with her, to make up to her for this terrible moment, to do anything in the world she wanted, to quit drinking just to make her happy.

The gun was coming up.

For a fraction of eternity I jeered at myself, my smartness, the good opinion I had of Dean Mallory, his ability to think fast, to write all sorts of smart clever things. I jeered because when it came to a showdown I . . . Then the thought came.

"Self-preservation, Sarakov?" The upward movement of the gun stopped. I had gained a respite.

"Yes, you are the only ones who know."

I laughed. It startled him, scared hell out of me. It was so sudden. "You're wrong, Michael, the police know," I added quickly for fear I'd lose the slight advantage. "I radioed the news ashore just before we came in here, gave them full particulars, asked them to check you with the F.B.I. You see I knew about the plans too."

"You lie!" he cried.

"It's true," Vicky said and started to cry. "It's true,

Michael."

There was another deep sigh from Rocky. That man had nerves of steel. Except for the low sighs and the barely perceptible sounds of movement I had heard he had not stirred.

"But the radio, just now," Michael said. "It did not know."

"The police wouldn't give that information out, wouldn't give you a chance to get away."

"But I'm getting away!" he boomed. "In less than an hour a boat will come for me. It is all arranged. Mallory, I intended killing you all." I smiled at his naive telling of that obvious fact. "However, since others know, it would be a useless killing. Yes, quite useless." He said that as if he were trying to convince himself.

"Wouldn't do you any good," Rocky said. "Only make it worse for you when . . ." He let his voice trail away and I said a little prayer of thanks for that. Sarakov was not in a mood to be goaded.

Sarakov ignored Rocky. "Mallory, if you will give me your word of honor that you will not attempt to arrest me, that you will leave this cabin in a few minutes and will take that man with you, then I will let you live," he said.

My throat felt like a dried fish-skin, my voice seemed to come from miles away.

"I agree—on my word of honor," I croaked.

The rigidness left his body—he put his automatic in his pocket and folded his arms. Vicky's hand found mine and gave it a reassuring squeeze. Bless her heart —if it hadn't been for her, my desire to save her, my insides would have been splattered all over the back of a chair by now—not that anyone outside of Vicky would give a damn, but they're mine and I'm quite attached to them.

I felt wobbly all over but tried not to show it. Little drops of perspiration were running down my back. I was glad it wasn't any worse than that.

My chair made a grating sound as I stood up. My nerves jumped.

"You are very positive of my guilt, aren't you?" he demanded.

"Yes."

"How did you discover the truth?"

"Little things," I replied.

"For instance?"

Vicky and Rocky were watching me, wondering what I would do. It seemed best to humor him. "You tried so hard to bring her back to life, tried when you were the only person present, except probably Desa and myself, who knew all about the reactions of curare. You went through that mockery, yet you knew she was dead."

"Ah," he said and then challenged, "You did not know it then, you thought of it afterward!"

"Yes. I also learned that you had a chance to steal some of the rubies before the contest."

"They were glass," he scoffed.

"But you managed to drop two of them near her body, that was clever of you, suggested an alibi, for if you had managed to get two of the stones you would not have had time to kill her."

There was approval in his eyes, or at least it seemed like approval to me. "Go on," he said.

"You washed your towels and hung them to dry in your bathroom."

"You are most observant, Mallory."

"Most writers are," I said. "Our observations make our stories."

"I underestimated you."

"That too was a mistake," I said boldly.

"Also your nerve," he said. "You have courage, my friend, nerves of steel. Too bad you do not use them. . . ." He sighed. "Perhaps some day I will come back with work for you to do."

"Your hair was wet from the fog when you asked us about Zamper," I added.

"I forgot about that," he admitted.

"And you used curare on him."

"I meant to drown him, but there was not time. I planned to hold him under the water until he was dead, only that fool Desa with his terror thwarted me."

"You shouldn't have taken the jewel box," I suggested. "It proved your interest in those plans." I looked at him a long moment. "I suppose you will take Grey's ten thousand dollars with you."

"Of course. It is little enough for the trouble I have had. Zamper stole the money from Grey. I simply took it away from him. That was how I lured him from his cabin."

He leaned back in his chair and surprised me by asking, "Are there no questions you would like to ask me?"

"Several," I replied. "Why did you lock Betty Potter in the refrigerator room?"

His laughter was low and long, rumbled. "I do not like her. She also might have remembered seeing me as I came out of your cabin, Miss Blaire. That was when I went for your knife."

"She didn't see you. If she did she'd have had it in print by now," Vicky said.

"Why did you think me dangerous so early in the evening?" I asked.

"You mean about the knife?"

"Yes."

"I began to have some respect for you, because you knew about curare."

"You were too openly willing to talk in the beginning," I said; "seemed to be too honest. Now I don't know what to believe."

"Does it matter?" he asked.

"No, but I did believe part of your story about Zara. I really thought you loved her."

"I did; all that was true about my early love. The image and the memories Zara conjured up for me meant more than life—gave me a reason for living. I fancied us as a team, a great team. At first she was very grateful and followed instructions. She was valuable to me, until she met this man Tricker. He turned her head. She cared more about being a great star than the cause for which she had sworn to give her life.

"She lied to me about those plans. She played a double game with Zamper. He became angry with her, was going to betray us all. He was angry with me because I had arranged to have him deported. I did not trust him, thought he would do better away from America and Zara. He was planning to turn against us, to expose our cause as so many rats have done. He wanted to stay in America, he had become soft."

"You say Zamper had planned to betray you both?"

"Yes. He promised to forget Zara's past if she gave him the plans and the ten thousand dollars. At the same time he had agreed to sell the story of Zara's life to Betty Potter. Zamper trusted the Potter woman. He was a fool. Potter told Zara what she was going to do. Zara flew into a rage and struck Potter. But you know that."

"Yes."

"She was very impetuous. In telling me of Zamper's treachery she did not realize that she was telling me of her own."

"Did she realize that you were going to kill her?"

"I think so. That is why she made a toast to death. She mocked me. She had burned the plans."

"She had courage."

"She also knew hate. She wanted to make me suffer. It was her way. My revenge was the Cossack way." He glanced at his watch and said, "It is time for you to go. I have your word."

He bowed gravely to Rocky and myself as we got up and walked to the door. As Vicky passed him he took her hand in his, looked deeply into her eyes and said, "Your eyes remind me of someone I lost long ago—true eyes, incapable of deceit. You will, perhaps, not think too unkindly of me?"

Michael Sarakov closed his eyes, his lower lip

trembled—it was time for us to go.

CHAPTER TWENTY

IT FELT GOOD TO BE out in the fresh air again. I took in a few deep breaths of good old salty ozone and felt better immediately. I don't mind admitting that Sarakov had scared the hell out of me—after all, a Mandarin robe and a sleepless night are darn poor equipment for a battle even if the former is all splashed over with gold dragons.

Vicky was crying softly beside me and I don't think Rocky was feeling any too damn cheerful himself, so I headed for her cabin. Once inside I took her in my arms and said, "You were wonderful, Vicky."

She dried her eyes, and in a small voice said, "I t-told you you'd n-need me—you big boob."

"I'll tell the world we sure needed you. If it hadn't been for you, we'd have been in a hell of a mess by now."

Rocky turned to me. "Y'know, I almost took a chance on making a jump at him."

That got a rise out of me.

"You mean you almost took a chance on my stomach. Well—I must say I'm glad that your native caution came to my rescue in time." The fellow grinned sheepishly.

"I'm sure glad I didn't. Say, d'you think he's going to commit suicide?"

"Oh, Dean, we must stop him!" Vicky cried.

"Darling—for his sake I hope so—but we are not going to interfere with his plans in any shape or form —as far as I'm concerned, all future interviews with him will be conducted over the long distance telephone. Your announcer, Dean Mallory, ex-investigator soon to be, aboard the good ship *Parrakeet.*"

Vicky put her arms around my neck and said that she thought maybe I was right. I hadn't any doubts about it myself.

Rocky began to look worried.

"Say, Chief . . ." I held up my hand.

"Rocky, don't Chief me any more. I've resigned—I don't feel worthy of the honor. You're elected. The mystery is solved—you get the credit and the glory, and I get a trip to Paradise. Fair enough?"

Rocky scratched his head.

"It's mighty swell of you, Chief—er, Mr. Mallory, but I don't know what to do about Sarakov."

"Ah! It's advice you want? That's different. I'll be glad to give it to you. You wish to know what to do about Michael Sarakov? My advice is nothing, absolutely nothing. Give him all the time he wants. When the fog lifts you may call out the coast guard, the militia and anything else you can think of and then make your arrest. I shall view the proceedings with great interest—from a safe distance."

"Guess you're right. I wouldn't want to get tough with him anyway."

I solemnly assured him that he was being very considerate.

I glanced at my watch and then suggested that we go on deck. If anything happened I was curious enough to want to see it in spite of all the advice I'd been giving to Rocky.

There was a golden ray of light streaking through a break in the fog. "For us," I said to Vicky. "Forever, I hope."

She gripped my arm. "You're not so bad."

Rocky's ear was cocked toward the shore. "Sounds like the sheriff's boat to me," he said.

Vicky broke away from us and ran down the deck. She pounded on the door of Sarakov's cabin and called, "They're coming from the shore, the sheriff's boat!" She ran back and threw herself into my arms. She looked across at Rocky. "I had to give him a chance."

We moved up the rail toward a group of people standing aimlessly about.

"Well—if it isn't Chu Chin Chow!" a smoky-voiced

blonde jeered. Then, "Oh, Mr. Mallory. Say, how about writing in a part for me in the *Blue Lagoon*? Sid said he'd like to use me only I wasn't the type. Imagine that—and me with my figure."

I told her that I wasn't much on figures and dragged Vicky farther up the deck. Rocky trailed along. We met Frank Lane.

"What gives?" he asked. "Can't we get out of here soon?"

"I think so," I answered as the sound of the boat grew closer.

Sarakov was on my mind. Had Vicky given him the signal for his suicide? Had he told us the truth when he said a boat was coming for him? Could he escape? I didn't see how it could be managed with the fog lifting so rapidly. Rocky would probably get hell for allowing him to kill himself. Well, that was Rocky's problem.

I couldn't see Sarakov doing a stretch in San Quentin or an institution for the criminally insane. No, he wouldn't submit. I thought of that gun and possible bloodshed, if he tried to shoot his way out. From what I remembered reading about Cossacks, they favored the "whoop and bang" method of making their worldly exits.

I made a decision but I was late. As I turned, determined to go to Sarakov's cabin and lock him in, the door opened. Sarakov stepped out, a great bear of a man in swimming trunks. There was no gun visible. His hands were empty but a knife was stuck through the belt of his trunks.

At the landing stage below I heard a motor dying to an underwater gurgle.

"It's the sheriff," Rocky said and stepped toward the ladder.

Sarakov came toward us, a wild primitive figure, his massive muscles rippling, his shock of long gray hair floating in the breeze, his great eyes staring straight ahead. As he reached us, Vicky cried, "Don't go on—the sheriff is here!"

Sarakov gave one hopeless look over the clearing bay. At the head of the ladder the sheriff appeared beside Rocky. Sarakov swung into action, leaped to the rail, then upon the end of a lifeboat and from there scrambled onto the main braces leading to the mast.

With a roar, Rocky went after him, leaped onto the end of the lifeboat, and clamped one hand on the Russian's ankle. The man instantly lashed out with his other foot and caught his assailant flush on the button. Rocky let go his hold and fell over backward into the lifeboat.

A feminine scream rent the air, a white arm flashed up and dealt my bloodhound a resounding slap in the face. A figure arose, draped a quilt about herself and climbed out of the boat—it was the "human doormat." I caught but a flash of this, then gave my whole attention to Sarakov.

Halfway up, the man twisted around and wedged his heels in a cross-bracing, then turned his head and looked down at us. By this time, everybody had crowded around, and stood gaping up at him.

When he spoke, a slow smile played about his lips.

"My friends," he said, "I have something of interest to show you." He reached into the belt of his swimming trunks, and pulled out the knife.

A gasp of horror went up from the crowd as Sarakov plunged the knife into the muscles of his left breast.

Suddenly I found his great eyes staring down at me— they seemed to be laughing. Slowly he turned his head and gazed into the water below.

Horrified, we watched his great chest heave spasmodically. For a few seconds he balanced on his precarious perch like some demigod turned to stone. Then the ship rolled and his huge body pitched head first into the sea. His arms were at his side. I saw the knife fall away, make a little splash of its own. Michael Sarakov— soldier of fortune, spy, idealist and murderer—had chosen his own method of escape.

CHAPTER TWENTY-ONE

AS SARAKOV PLUNGED head first into the sea several women fainted. The lustier and more morbid ran to the rail to see what had happened to his body. Vicky was sobbing violently. I didn't feel so good myself. Rocky climbed out of the lifeboat, a little white around the gills.

"Why did you let him get away?" the sheriff demanded, very much annoyed.

"That," I said, "is quite a story. Have Rocky tell it to you some day. Rocky tried to stop him, he did all that he could. If he had done more we would have been cold mutton, right now."

"Well—" the sheriff began somewhat grudgingly.

Something in my brain clicked. Things had been happening very quickly and yet there had been a sense of incompleteness about it, a definite something lacking. Sarakov had stood in the rigging, had stabbed himself melodramatically. We had all supposed that he had used curare. There had, however, been no spurt of blood from that self-inflicted wound. He had stood there for a moment looking down, his eyes had laughed at me as if he were enjoying some huge joke at my expense. He had gone down head first with his arms at his side, had plunged into the water in a perfect dive, well calculated to give him great depth from the plunge.

I ran across the deck to the opposite rail. The *Parrakeet* lay a few hundred feet away. I waited patiently; I saw her give a slight tilting heave to one side. I gave a deep grunt of satisfaction as I saw a figure crawl up over her side and drop into the cockpit. I had been right, after all. Sarakov had planned a clever escape, was on the *Parrakeet* waiting for my return, waiting to force me to carry him away, to the boat he had mentioned or perhaps to Mexico.

He had been laughing at me, perhaps right then as he lay in the cockpit of the *Parrakeet* he was laughing at the way he had duped me. I had played into his hands, I would be the instrument of his escape. The gun and its muzzle waved in front of my eyes again. I should have been afraid, instead I was mad, filled with a hot and burning resentment. The nerve of the man! To think me a fool, to use my boat the *Parrakeet* as his means of escape!

Rage, hot and quick, surged over me, robbed me of my good sense, my native caution, my fear of the man and his great physical strength. My course of action would have been so clearly defined were it not for my fury. Make a fool out of me, would he? Use me and the *Parrakeet*, eh? Perhaps force me to do his will with my own gun in the cabin. No! I'd get to him before he found that gun, I'd show him that I was a match for him, that I had seen through the cunning of his plan.

Vicky came and stood beside me as I undid the Mandarin robe. "Get Rocky, the sheriff, men, the *Parrakeet*," I said as I pulled the robe away from my shoulders, slipped out of the pajama top, kicked off the slippers and dove overboard.

As I went down I heard her gasp and caught a yip from Shang.

My truce with Sarakov was over. I was boiling mad. I'd show him!

He was on the floor of the cockpit as I pulled myself over the gunwale. His eyes widened in unbelief, he started to push himself away from the floor. I slid over the edge of the deck down upon him, hoping to knock some of the wind out of him by the impact of my weight. He was strong; I'd have little chance against him; but I didn't care. I'd been itching for a fight and this was it. My body was wet, his hands slipped down over my back as he tried to get me into a bear hug. I heard him grunt. His fingers dug into the soft flesh just above my hips. He rolled and tossed me away from him.

"The clever Mr. Mallory," he sneered, "knows too

much."

We clinched again, slipped on the deck. I tried to get in a telling blow but our quarters were cramped. His arms tightened about me. I could feel the water trickling down my legs. His elbow had gone under my chin, was forcing my head up and back, his knee was coming up, he was going to put me out as quickly as possible, perhaps break my neck first. I did all that I could to break that hold, my muscles strained; his knee kept coming up and up; I tried to shift our balance, managed to throw him a little to one side; his grip lessened for a minute but he let out a roar of rage. I turned the tables, jerked my knee up quickly and let him have it in the stomach. He gave a great exhaustive roar and staggered backward. His eyes were bloodshot, his face contorted. I sensed my finish. He was ready for a new charge which would be the end of Dean Mallory.

Then the miracle of Lee Wing happened. Sarakov had backed toward the companionway. Lee Wing cracked him over the head with an iron skillet—not a romantic means of rescue perhaps but terribly effective. There was a hollow sound, like the crushing of a dry gourd. Sarakov sagged to the deck just as the launch bumped the side of the *Parrakeet*.

They came aboard. Rocky had brought my pajamas and robe. "She said you'd need these," Rocky said, tossing them to me.

Sarakov was groaning. The sheriff clamped the handcuffs to his wrists and stood up to face me. "That was fast clever thinking, Mallory," he said.

I had slipped into my pajamas and robe, had recovered somewhat from the exertion and strain. "Drop me off at the yacht on the way in, will you? I want to bring a guest over here for breakfast."

"You bling um lady?" Lee Wing asked.

At my nod, he took his skillet and went back to the galley.

When I climbed the ladder on the yacht Vicky sprang

into my arms and began to sob. "Oh, Dean, you're such a nice fool!" she said between gasps. "Are you all right?"

Everything was all right then. I forgot the ache of my muscles, the sharp sting of the scratches on my side, everything but the fact that Vicky was telling me again in her way that she wanted to be Mrs. Mallory.

Betty Potter came plunging down the deck all a-dither with excitement. "What goes on, Dean? Have I missed something?"

"Oh no—nothing at all. Since you've been in hiding Zamper has been murdered, we've found out who killed him and Zara. Sarakov pretended to commit suicide and tried a clever plan to escape."

"And Mr. Mallory got him," Rocky said proudly.

Her eyes very nearly popped out of her head and into her open mouth. "Well, for pity's sake, tell me about it!"

"Sorry, Betty, it's not my story. Talk to the man who solved the riddle. You know Rocky. I'm sure he'll be glad to give you all the details."

She made a dive for Rocky, clutched at his arm, but Rocky decided flatly, "I'll have to talk to the sheriff first."

Betty started to splutter. Rocky gave her one withering glance and turned toward the bar. The general movement had been in that direction. I had seen Shang waddle in there and went after him.

Some egg had put Shang on the bar. I made a grab for him. The little cuss turned and snapped at me.

"Better have a bracer," Rocky suggested.

Such is the force of habit and suggestion that I reached for a long drink, ready to surround it, when I suddenly remembered. Slowly I pushed the glass away, far away out of my reach and turned from the bar.

Vicky's eyes were like bright beacons. There was a light there that's worth millions to a man. I hope I'll always see it and if I don't I'll know it's my fault.

Sid came tearing in. "What has happened, Dean? Tell me quick!"

"It's all over, Sid. Sarakov was the murderer. He tried

to escape but has been caught."

Sid gasped and reached for my abandoned drink. Frank Lane, St. Denis and Naomi joined us. Naomi put an arm about Vicky, who looked beautifully happy.

I said to Frank and Naomi, "Sid has something to tell you—haven't you, Sid?"

"What?"

I leaned over and whispered as he returned to his drink, "Want your marriage kept secret?"

He choked into his glass. When he looked up I knew his memory had revived.

"Frank," he said, "I was only kidding about putting some other director on *Blue Lagoon*. You're the man for me. And, Naomi, you can play the lead opposite Basil, if you want the part."

She put an arm through his, "Of course I want it, Sid. Now I have a surprise for you. Basil and I are going to be married."

He pouted. "I don't know whether I—"

I knew what he was thinking. "Of course you like the idea," I said. "Think of the publicity—Happiness comes out of Tragedy, etc."

He considered a moment. "It's good," he said. "Where's Betty Potter?"

She, of course, was right there.

A few minutes later we were ready to leave. A fast boat was plowing through the waters racing into the bay. "Reporters," I said to Vicky.

Rocky, his face cracked with a broad grin, turned to say goodbye. "I'll see you soon," he promised. "I can't be a four-flusher, Mr. Mallory. I've told the Chief you did all the work."

"And I'll tell the reporters you're a liar. You'd better keep 'em here. I'm going back to the Mainland to arrange for a wedding."

Betty was full of feature story, ready to rush to a telegraph key.

Rocky reached down to pat Shang just as we started

down the ladder. In a dinghy below a sailor waited to row us over to the *Parrakeet*.

Grey came forward with a soggy manila envelope in his hand. "Thanks," he said to Rocky.

"Keep quiet!" Rocky growled. "If the sheriff had found that dough it would all come out about the plans and all."

"What goes on?" I asked.

"Rocky found this envelope sticking out of Sarakov's swimming trunks, rescued it and returned the ten thousand dollars to me."

"Nice going, Rocky. Smart fellow!" I turned to Grey. "Don't let Betty Potter get wind of it."

Betty crowded in on us. I might have known that we couldn't get away without a farewell blast.

"Be sure to get a copy of next Sunday's *New York Sphere*, Mr. Mallory. It's going to have the cutest story in it."

"I shall be delighted to read it, Betty." I let Vicky go down the ladder ahead of me. I moved back to the top step, ignoring the freshening breeze. "You might add to your story that Mr. and Mrs. Mallory will be spending their honeymoon on the good ship *Parrakeet*." I let that sink in. "Also something about an icebox and a blackmail story you bought from one of the victims which will explain why you were locked in the refrigerator, and don't forget to add that you were indirectly the cause of the murder."

I made her a deep, sweeping bow—I shouldn't have been so courtly. Something happened to my pajama cord, sleezy silk slithered down my legs—at my feet lay a pair of green silk pajama pants.

A howl went up from the crowd.

With as much carefree abandon as I could muster, I stepped out of the damned pajamas and followed the future Mrs. Mallory down the ladder.

THE END

Resurrected Press Books in *The Chief Inspector Pointer Mystery* Series

MYSTERIES BY ANNE AUSTIN

Murder at Bridge

When an afternoon bridge party attended by some of Hamilton's leading citizens ends with the hostess being murdered in her boudoir, Special Investigator Dundee of the District Attorney's office is called in. But one of the attendees is guilty? There are plenty of suspects: the victim's former lover, her current suitor, the retired judge who is being blackmailed, the victim's maid who had been horribly disfigured accidentally by the murdered woman, or any of the women who's husbands had flirted with the victim. Or was she murdered by an outsider whose motive had nothing to do with the town of Hamilton. Find the answer in... **Murder at Bridge**

One Drop of Blood

When Dr. Koenig, head of Mayfield Sanitarium is murdered, the District Attorney's Special Investigator, "Bonnie" Dundee must go undercover to find the killer. Were any of the inmates of the asylum insane enough to have committed the crime? Or, was it one of the staff, motivated by jealousy? And what was is the secret in the murdered man's past. Find the answer in... **One Drop of Blood**

AVAILABLE FROM RESURRECTED PRESS!

GEMS OF MYSTERY
LOST JEWELS FROM A MORE ELEGANT AGE

Three wonderful tales of mystery from some of the best known writers of the period before the First World War -

A foggy London night, a Russian princess who steals jewels, a corpse; a mysterious murder, an opera singer, and stolen pearls; two young people who crash a masked ball only to find themselves caught up in a daring theft of jewels; these are the subjects of this collection of entertaining tales of love, jewels, and mystery. This collection includes:

- **In the Fog - by Richard Harding Davis's**

- **The Affair at the Hotel Semiramis - by A.E.W. Mason**

- **Hearts and Masks - Harold MacGrath**

AVAILABLE FROM RESURRECTED PRESS!

THE EDWARDIAN DETECTIVES
LITERARY SLEUTHS OF THE EDWARDIAN ERA

The exploits of the great Victorian Detectives, Poe's C. Auguste Dupin, Gaboriau's Lecoq, and most famously, Arthur Conan Doyle's Sherlock Holmes, are well known. But what of those fictional detectives that came after, those of the Edwardian Age? The period between the death of Queen Victoria and the First World War had been called the Golden Age of the detective short story, but how familiar is the modern reader with the sleuths of this era? And such an extraordinary group they were, including in their numbers an unassuming English priest, a blind man, a master of disguises, a lecturer in medical jurisprudence, a noble woman working for Scotland Yard, and a savant so brilliant he was known as "The Thinking Machine."

To introduce readers to these detectives, Resurrected Press has assembled a collection of stories featuring these and other remarkable sleuths in The Edwardian Detectives.

- The Case of Laker, Absconded by Arthur Morrison
- The Fenchurch Street Mystery by Baroness Orczy
- The Crime of the French Café by Nick Carter
- The Man with Nailed Shoes by R Austin Freeman
- The Blue Cross by G. K. Chesterton
- The Case of the Pocket Diary Found in the Snow by Augusta Groner
- The Ninescore Mystery by Baroness Orczy
- The Riddle of the Ninth Finger by Thomas W. Hanshew
- The Knight's Cross Signal Problem by Ernest Bramah

- The Problem of Cell 13 by Jacques Futrelle
- The Conundrum of the Golf Links by Percy James Brebner
- The Silkworms of Florence by Clifford Ashdown
- The Gateway of the Monster by William Hope Hodgson
- The Affair at the Semiramis Hotel by A. E. W. Mason
- The Affair of the Avalanche Bicycle & Tyre Co., LTD by Arthur Morrison

RESURRECTED PRESS CLASSIC MYSTERY CATALOGUE

The Middle of Things
Ravensdene Court
Scarhaven Keep
The Orange-Yellow Diamond
The Middle Temple Murder
The Tallyrand Maxim
The Borough Treasurer
In the Mayor's Parlour
The Saftey Pin

R. Austin Freeman
*The Mystery of 31 New Inn from the Dr. Thorndyke
Series*
*John Thorndyke's Cases from the Dr. Thorndyke
Series*
The Red Thumb Mark from The Dr. Thorndyke Series
The Eye of Osiris from The Dr. Thorndyke Series
A Silent Witness from the Dr. John Thorndyke Series
The Cat's Eye from the Dr. John Thorndyke Series
*Helen Vardon's Confession: A Dr. John Thorndyke
Story*
As a Thief in the Night: A Dr. John Thorndyke Story
*Mr. Pottermack's Oversight: A Dr. John Thorndyke
Story*
*Dr. Thorndyke Intervenes: A Dr. John Thorndyke
Story*
The Singing Bone: The Adventures of Dr. Thorndyke
The Stoneware Monkey: A Dr. John Thorndyke Story
*The Great Portrait Mystery, and Other Stories: A
Collection of Dr. John Thorndyke and Other Stories*
The Penrose Mystery: A Dr. John Thorndyke Story
The Uttermost Farthing: A Savant's Vendetta

Arthur Griffiths
The Passenger From Calais
The Rome Express

Fergus Hume
The Mystery of a Hansom Cab
The Green Mummy
The Silent House
The Secret Passage

Edgar Jepson
The Loudwater Mystery

A. E. W. Mason
At the Villa Rose

A. A. Milne
The Red House Mystery
Baroness Emma Orczy
The Old Man in the Corner

Edgar Allan Poe
The Detective Stories of Edgar Allan Poe

Arthur J. Rees
The Hampstead Mystery
The Shrieking Pit
The Hand In The Dark
The Moon Rock
The Mystery of the Downs

Mary Roberts Rinehart
Sight Unseen and The Confession

Dorothy L. Sayers
Whose Body?

Sir William Magnay
The Hunt Ball Mystery

Mabel and Paul Thorne
The Sheridan Road Mystery

Louis Tracy
The Strange Case of Mortimer Fenley
The Albert Gate Mystery
The Bartlett Mystery
The Postmaster's Daughter
The House of Peril
The Sandling Case: What Would You Have Done?
Charles Edmonds Walk
The Paternoster Ruby

John R. Watson
The Mystery of the Downs
The Hampstead Mystery

Edgar Wallace
The Daffodil Mystery
The Crimson Circle

Carolyn Wells
Vicky Van
The Man Who Fell Through the Earth
In the Onyx Lobby
Raspberry Jam
The Clue
The Room with the Tassels
The Vanishing of Betty Varian
The Mystery Girl
The White Alley
The Curved Blades
Anybody but Anne
The Bride of a Moment
Faulkner's Folly
The Diamond Pin
The Gold Bag
The Mystery of the Sycamore
The Come Backy

Raoul Whitfield
Death in a Bowl

And much more!
Visit ResurrectedPress.com
for our complete catalogue

About Resurrected Press

A division of Intrepid Ink, LLC, Resurrected Press is dedicated to bringing high quality, vintage books back into publication. See our entire catalogue and find out more at www.ResurrectedPress.com.

About Intrepid Ink, LLC

Intrepid Ink, LLC provides full publishing services to authors of fiction and non-fiction books, eBooks and websites. From editing to formatting, from publishing to marketing, Intrepid Ink gets your creative works into the hands of the people who want to read them. Find out more at www.IntrepidInk.com.

www.ingramcontent.com/pod-product-compliance
Lightning Source LLC
Chambersburg PA
CBHW071313250626
47159CB00004B/1406